GRISTLE

MARK ALLEN

&

DERRIC MILLER

DEDICATION

This one is for all of the angels and demons in our lives. Because of them, we'll always have stories to tell.

ACKNOWLEDGMENTS

Special thanks to Jamie Sheffield, not only for letting us borrow one of his characters for a cameo, but for some awesome beta feedback that helped us make a good book even better.

PROLOGUE

Jack Colter, his wife Trisha, and fourteen-year-old son Kevin sat at their kitchen table, together as a family, dinner spread out before them. It was their evening ritual; not quite sacred, but important enough that they tried to do it as many nights as possible. This being Friday night and nobody had felt like cooking, they had ordered pizza—extra pepperoni and anchovies—from Grub's Pub and Grill over in Bloomingdale. Usually they spent the time catching up with each other on the day's events, planning a vacation, debating politics or religion, and just generally bonding. Had anyone asked, Jack would have readily told them that they were a close-knit family and having supper together every night was one of the reasons why.

But tonight, nobody was eating. Because instead of strengthening family bonds, they were being tortured by actual bonds. Their ankles were duct-taped to the legs of their chairs, their hands lashed together behind them with black zip ties. Jack tried to wiggle his hands but their captor knew what he was doing. The ties refused to yield, cutting so deep into his wrists that circulation was sluggish. He could barely feel his fingers. The pungent tang of fear-sweat permeated the room and as Jack looked around at his family, he saw their faces filled with dread. He wondered what they saw on his face when they looked at him. If fear wasn't carved into every line of his features, it should have been—he was scared to death.

Trisha was sobbing and Kevin was crying but Jack tempered his fear with rage as he glared at the man who had invaded their home. Despite living in one of the quietest towns in the Adirondack Park, the Colters still kept their doors locked at night. But the lock on the front door had proven no match for a .45 caliber bullet. The intruder had burst in wearing a black ski mask, brandishing a 9mm automatic in one hand and a Colt .45 in the other. The handle of the Colt was made of what looked like walnut and there was a dragon carved into the wood, along with five notches.

The two weapons were all the man needed to hold the family hostage. With guns aimed at his loved ones, Jack had done nothing as the invader bound them, his intent still unclear. Jack just fervently prayed that whatever that intent turned out to be, murder wasn't part of the equation. Whatever else happened, Jack reckoned he could live with it as long as his family came out the other side still alive.

The masked man dangled the 9mm in front of Jack's face. The light from the elk antler chandelier hanging above the table bounced off the reflective steel and stabbed at Jack's eyes in silver flashes. The intruder waggled the pistol like a taunt as he growled, "Bet you'd like to have this piece of hot lead hardware right about now, huh?"

Jack didn't reply. His look said it all.

But his look wasn't good enough for the masked man. He leaned into Jack's face until their noses were tip to tip and screamed, "Answer the fuckin' question!" The man didn't articulate a threat, but he didn't need to. It was

3

very clear to Jack that if he failed to answer, there would be serious consequences.

"Yes," Jack whispered.

"What?" the man yelled.

"YES!" Jack yelled back and instantly regretted it. The invader could interpret the yell as defiance and shift from verbal taunts to physical punishment. *Get a grip, Jack. Don't give this maniac a reason to go kill crazy.*

"Yes … what?" the man mocked. His face was hidden under the ski mask, but Jack imagined the asshole was smirking.

"Yes, I'd like to have that gun right about now," Jack said, following the script. He was an actor in a dark family tragedy being directed by a madman with firepower.

The man slammed the 9mm down on the table in front of Jack so hard that the anchovies jumped off the pizza's congealing cheese and the salt shaker tipped over, spilling its crystalline contents.

"Well, why didn't you say so?" he asked. "It's gonna cost you, though, and the price is a real motherfucker."

Keeping the .45 tucked tight against Trisha's temple, the man whipped a folding knife from out of his pocket. Jack experienced a marrow-freezing moment of panic as the masked man flicked open the blade, imagining the razor edge sinking into his wife's throat. But the only thing the man slashed open were the plastic ties binding Jack's hands. The ease with which the plastic parted let Jack know just how sharp that knife was.

He rubbed his wrists, raw from where the plastic straps had gouged into his flesh. The 9mm lay tantalizing before him, looking like lethal salvation in a hard steel package. But he knew it was an illusion. Their captor had a .45 pressed to his wife's head. No matter how fast he grabbed up the gun, it wouldn't be fast enough to prevent the man from putting a bullet in Trisha's skull. So he just left the 9mm laying there, making sure his hands went nowhere near it. The man was looking for a reason to kill and Jack didn't want to give him one.

As if to prove the point, the man suddenly ground the muzzle of the .45 into Trisha's temple and snarled, "I want to kill your wife. Or fuck her. I can't decide which. Maybe both. In that order."

Trisha gasped in terror. Kevin began crying again. Jack thought his son's face looked too young to bear the horror he was now facing.

"No!" Jack begged. He desperately wanted

to do something, anything, to spare his family further trauma. "Please … don't."

"Well, asshole, that's all up to you." The man's voice was one of amused malice, the cat toying with the mouse. "You see, I'm gonna give you a chance to save your wife."

"Anything! I'll do anything! Just please don't hurt her." Jack practically babbled his eagerness to do whatever it took, whatever the madman wanted.

"Glad to hear it," the man said. "Now, pick up the gun."

"What?"

"You heard me. Pick up the gun."

Jack glanced down at the gun lying in front of him, then back up at the man. Back down at the gun. Back to the man.

His hesitation seemed to piss the man off. "Are you fuckin' deaf?" he snarled. "Are you having trouble hearing? Pick. Up. The. Fucking. Gun."

Jack's hand trembled as he obeyed the command. But once his sweaty palm gripped the cold steel, it took everything he had not to just shoot the bastard. In the movies, right about now the hero would snap-shoot a bullet right between the villain's eyes, ending the terror and putting the world right once again.

But this was no movie and he for damn sure was no hero.

"Now tuck the barrel under your chin nice and tight," the masked man said. "Right there above the lump in your throat."

There actually was a lump in his throat. Jack swallowed hard and did as ordered. The metal of the gun's muzzle felt surprisingly cool against his skin.

"Good boy," the man crooned. "Now pull the trigger."

Jack gaped at him in horror.

"Now!" the man shouted.

Jack just sat there, frozen with fear.

"I said, now!" The man brought the .45 back—for some reason, it seemed to Jack like the dragon etched into the walnut grips was writhing like a snake—and then whipped it forward, striking Trisha across the brow. Not hard enough to knock her out, but the blow split her skin and blood ran down her face. She cried out in pain.

"Do it!" the man snarled. "Or so help me, God, I will bash her fuckin' brains out all over this pizza."

Jack wasn't sure when his tears had started, but he suddenly realized they were streaming down his face in wet mockery of the blood streaking Trisha's features. *Husband and wife, 'til death do us part,* he crazily thought. He slowly curled his shaking finger around the trigger and pulled it back halfway. Another three pounds of pressure would drop the firing pin. Another three pounds and he would feel—or, more likely, *not* feel—a bullet burn through his brain. Another three pounds and he would save his wife.

But those three pounds proved impossible. His trembling finger simply refused to override his self-preservation instincts.

With the trigger locked at the halfway point, Jack let out a sigh tinged with desperation. "I can't," he said weakly. He avoided his wife's eyes, not wanting to see his shame mirrored there.

"Bad news for the missus then," the man said. "All right, let's keep this simple. I'm gonna rattle off a five count. If I reach five and you haven't put a bullet through your head, I'm gonna put one through your wife's. Got it? Whether she lives or dies is entirely in your hands. Right here, right now, you are God. Life or death. The choice is all yours."

He paused to let it sink in, eyes glittering with menace behind the ski mask. Then he started the countdown. "One."

Kevin struggled against his bonds as he screamed, "Dad, do something!"

Jack tried again, straining to pull the trigger. *Don't do it!* shouted the primal, reptilian side of his brain. *You have to do it!* the emotional side countered. His hand shook like a meth addict with Parkinson's. But the trigger remained static.

"Two."

Beneath the crimson streaks, Trisha's face was pale white. "Jack?" she whispered, voice quivering with fear.

Jack couldn't bear to look at her. He kept his eyes fixed on their tormenter. "Why are you doing this to us?" he shouted. "Why?"

The chilling answer offered no comfort. "Because it's fun," the man said. "Three."

"Please stop!" Jack thought he had known panic before but it was nothing compared to the frantic horror he was feeling now.

"You can make me stop," the man replied. "Just pull the trigger." He paused a moment, apparently for dramatic effect, then intoned, "Four."

Jack glanced at his wife just in time to see a terrible serenity come over her face, as if she had accepted her fate. Accepted the fact that her husband would not save her. She squeezed her eyes shut and in a quiet voice murmured, "Jack, honey…"

"No no no no no no…" The single word spilled from Jack's lips again and again, his frantic mind caught in a nightmarish mental loop.

The masked man suddenly abandoned his conversational tone and switched to bellowing rage. "I'LL DO IT! I'll PAINT THIS PLACE WITH HER BRAINS! PULL THE FUCKING TRIGGER! I'll DO IT! I SWEAR TO GOD I'LL FUCKING DO IT!" His angry voice bounced off the walls and seemed to consume the room with a reverberating echo.

Kevin added to the chaotic soundscape by shrieking, "Dad! Dad! Dad!"

Yet somehow, someway, in what was maybe meant to be an act of mercy from God but was anything but, Jack clearly heard Trisha's last words.

"I love you, Jack."

He looked into her eyes and saw the forgiveness there and his heart shattered into a thousand jagged pieces.

"Five," his tormentor said, his tone infused with the finality of a death knell. Unlike Jack, he had no trouble pulling the trigger.

The gunshot sounded louder than the

screams of ten thousand angels to Jack's stricken mind. Trisha's head snapped to the side under the hammering point-blank impact of the .45 slug. The side of her skull disintegrated and sprayed a clumpy mess of crimson brains all over Kevin's sobbing face. In a single heartbeat, with a single pull of a trigger, she was transformed from loyal wife and loving mother into a lifeless corpse.

Chuckling evilly, the masked man took the 9mm away from Jack, which was easy to do since he was just sitting there slumped in shock and horror. His mind had started shutting down, unable to process the fact that the woman he loved had just died because he had been too much of a coward to save her. *Congratulations, Jack, you just killed your wife.*

He could take no more. His mind flicked a switch and he slithered down the dark hole into unconsciousness.

He never saw the masked man leave or heard his final taunting words.

"Good luck getting over this one, Jack. God hates a fuckin' coward."

CHAPTER 1

AT THE GATES OF HELL

Jack sat alone in the front pew of the church, staring up at the wooden cross that dominated the wall behind the pulpit. This being a Baptist church rather than Catholic, the cross was just a cross, not a crucifix—there was no impaled Christ. Jack was thankful for that. He understood the whole "Jesus died on the cross for the sins of the world" thing, but there had been more than enough blood and violence in his life, so he was glad that he didn't have to come to church on Sundays and look at an innocent man nailed to a hunk of wood.

A purple banner stretched above the cross and greeted anyone who entered the sanctuary with "Welcome to Vesper Falls Baptist Church." It was a simple banner and a simple greeting, but this was a simple country church. Nestled in the northern Adirondacks between the quaint mountain town of Saranac Lake and the bustling city of Plattsburgh, Vesper Falls boasted a population of 803. Maybe five percent of that population showed up for Sunday morning worship, double that on Easter and Christmas. As towns went, Vesper Falls wasn't particularly religious and Jack suspected even those who attended church viewed it more as a social gathering than anything to do with true faith. Not that there was anything wrong with that. In Jack's experience, true faith usually just ended up in bitter disappointment.

Jack sat on the pew and listened to the congregants in the foyer as they headed home for Sunday dinners with family, voices full of hope and joy, a stark contrast to the bleak and blackened thoughts scorching his own mind. It was probably good his neighbors couldn't see the darkness caged within him. He didn't hate them or anything like that, but he sometimes couldn't help but resent them for their normalcy.

But while he might not have hated his neighbors, there was someone—or rather, Someone—that he *had* learned to hate.

Staring up at the cross, Jack whispered, "You son of a bitch, you let me kill her."

A hand gripped his shoulder. Jack jumped up out of the pew and spun around, hands raised for combat or defense. His heart rate immediately doubled.

Pastor Larry Wainwright held up his hands, palms out to show there was no threat. "Whoa! Hold on, Jack, it's just me." With the thinning hair and expanding paunch of middle age and wearing a tweed sports coat, Larry looked more like a professor than a pastor. Someone who should be expounding on the phallic symbolism of *Moby Dick* to a college class rather than preaching about the follies of Jonah and how running from Jehovah just landed you in whale vomit.

Jack lowered his arms. "Sorry," he said. "You caught me with my head somewhere else."

"No need to apologize to me, but I'm betting the word that just went zipping through your brain wasn't exactly church-appropriate,"

Larry said, "so you might owe God a 'sorry.'" His voice was rich and earthy with a dulcet tone that served him well behind the pulpit.

"Yeah, well, me and God aren't exactly on the best of terms these days," Jack said. "I'm kind of holding a grudge over the whole dead wife thing."

"No time like the present to patch up that problem," Larry replied.

Let it go, preacher. Jack could feel himself growing agitated. He made a noise in his throat that might have been a growl, might have been something more benign, and even he wasn't sure which. "It's not always that simple," he said. "God or not, sometimes life just sucks." He almost added the word *dick* but caught himself at the last second.

Larry chuckled. "Life sucks. That would make a great sermon title." He paused for a moment before turning more serious. "Honestly, Jack, I get what you're saying. Twenty years ago my wife died giving birth to Holly, leaving me to raise a baby girl on my own, and then two years ago Holly was killed on that hike. So yeah, I'd say I know a thing or two about the rough stuff."

Jack was surprised. Larry so rarely spoke of the past that it was sometimes easy to forget that the man had his own tragic cross to bear. Jack had one gravestone to visit at Union Cemetery. Larry had two.

Wonder if he drinks away the pain every night too.

"Difference is," Jack said, "that cougar killed Holly before you even had a chance to do anything about it. You didn't have the option of saving her. I can't say the same thing about Trisha."

"You were faced with an impossible choice."

"Shouldn't have been a choice at all," Jack snapped. "The only reason it was impossible is because I'm a damn coward." Suddenly he didn't give a crap about cussing in church.

"Jack, listen—"

But Jack put up his hand to cut him off. "No offense, Larry, but I really don't want to talk about it anymore."

"Okay, what do you want to talk about? I assume there's a reason you're still here."

Jack looked down at his feet, shoulders slumped. "Kevin. He gets out tomorrow. I have to pick him up at eleven." Just saying his son's name made Jack hurt in ways he couldn't even describe. Trisha might have been the one that died that horrible night, but she was not the only victim.

When Jack looked up, he saw surprise on the preacher's face. "I thought he'd be in there longer…" Larry's voice trailed off, letting the sentence hang awkwardly.

Jack knew where the awkwardness came from. Knew that what Larry was really saying was *He should have been in there longer.* Vesper Falls was a small town and they did not easily forget—or forgive—crimes against their own. "He was sentenced as a minor," Jack explained, "which means they could only hold him until he turned eighteen, which he did a few days ago."

Larry nodded. "Well, that makes sense." He paused, then added, "As long as a man is truly sorry, the sins of his past shouldn't be held against him."

Jack almost laughed. It was obvious Larry wasn't really talking about Kevin. Sometimes the preacher could be as subtle as a sledgehammer.

"Anyway," Larry continued, "what happens next? Between the two of you, I mean."

"He's my son," Jack replied. "Nothing I would like more than to put this rough patch behind us. Just not sure that's even possible at this point."

Larry put an encouraging hand on Jack's shoulder. "That's good to hear. Everyone deserves a second chance."

"Yeah, that's what I wanted to talk to you about. I'm kind of at a loss on how to move forward with Kevin."

"When's the last time you saw him?"

Jack lowered his head again, as if the floor of the sanctuary held answers to the problems of his life, and said, "The day he went to juvie."

He heard a quick intake of breath from Larry, followed by an incredulous, "They locked him up three years ago and you never went to visit him?"

Jack looked up and gave him a cynical smile. "Oh, I went. Every Saturday morning, religiously. But he refused my visits. Every single one of them."

Larry said nothing, obviously at a loss for words. Jack filled the silence by saying, "My son hates me." Though he had faced that fact a long time ago, it was the first time Jack had uttered the words aloud. It felt like a confession … a confession that hurt like hell.

Larry stared at Jack for several long seconds, unblinking, apparently pondering something. Finally he seemed to reach a decision. "Maybe

I do have something to help," he said, pulling a set of keys from his pocket. He removed one of the keys from the ring and offered it to Jack.

"What's that?" Jack asked.

"It's called a key," Larry said, mouth quirking up in amusement.

"Well, yeah, I know that."

"Hey, you asked. But to answer the question you were really asking, it's the key to my cabin in Scar Lake. Why don't you and Kevin head up there for a few days, do some deer hunting together, try to reconnect?"

Jack smiled, and it felt out of place on his face. "Not a bad idea. Thanks, Larry, I appreciate it."

"There is one catch," Larry said. "You'll have to share the place with another father and son."

The caveat didn't exactly thrill Jack. He figured he and Kevin stood a better chance at rebuilding a bond if they were alone. Hard to have heart to heart chats and spill your emotional guts with strangers around. But it didn't look like he had much of a choice. "Anyone I know?" he asked.

"Paul Rickson. Moved here a few months ago. Know him?"

"Just from crossing paths with him down at

the store or here at church. Seems like a nice enough guy."

"He is a nice guy," Larry said. "A nice guy with a seventeen year-old son named Tom who suffers from anorexia. Been away in rehab for the past six months and just came home last week. Paul said he'd like to get away, spend some time with his son, so I gave him a key to my lodge."

Jack still would have preferred to have the cabin to themselves, but as the saying went, you can't look a gift horse in the mouth. At least it sounded like the Ricksons weren't assholes, so sharing the cabin wouldn't be an unpleasant experience. Jack mulled it over for a few more moments, then said, "It's fine. Really. I appreciate it."

"Are you sure? You could always go some other time." Larry almost seemed to be regretting his decision.

"No, the sooner the better," Jack said.

Larry hesitated for just another sliver of a second, then nodded. "Okay, I'll call Paul's cell and let him know you're coming."

Surprised, Jack said, "You get cell service out there?"

"Right around the cabin, yes," Larry said. "Anywhere else but the cabin, you're better off using a carrier pigeon. Now let me draw you a map so you can get on out of here."

As Larry shuffled off in search of pen and paper, Jack glanced back up at the cross he had so recently cursed. He considered offering an apology, but then shook his head. *Not a chance in hell.*

******

A few minutes later, Jack exited the church with Larry's key in his pocket and a map in his hand. He stood at the bottom of the terrace for a moment and enjoyed the crisp sensation of the cool autumn air kissing his skin. The sun burned high and bright in the cloudless sky. It was the kind of day that reminded him why fall was his favorite season.

He breathed deeply, inhaling the earthy scents and the fresh mountain breeze, then moved across the parking lot at a brisk clip. Since Larry lived in the parsonage next door, Jack's Jeep Wrangler was the only vehicle left in the parking lot. The Jeep was "murdered out," meaning it was black from roof to rims. He had given the Wrangler to Trisha as an anniversary present a few months before she died and back then it had been bright yellow. Following her murder, Jack had blackened the

Jeep, partly as part of his mourning process, but mostly just because it better matched his somber mood.

Once settled in the driver's seat, Jack closed the door, but didn't start the engine. Instead, he swiveled his head three hundred and sixty degrees, then checked and double-checked his mirrors. Satisfied there were no witnesses to his imminent transgression, he leaned over and retrieved a flask from the glove box.

Really? some inner voice chided. *Right here in the church parking lot?*

That voice was always chastising him, but he had learned how to ignore it. Or rather, how to drown it. He uncapped the flask and took a slug, grimacing as the bourbon scorched his throat. *Sweet liquid fire,* he thought, twisting the cap back on and tossing the flask back in the glove compartment. He swiped his mouth with the back of his hand, then started the engine and shifted the Jeep into gear.

As he swung the Jeep out of its parking spot, the cross on the crest of the church steeple blocked the sun and splayed a cruciform shadow across the hood of the vehicle. From Jack's vantage point, looking through the windshield, the cross appeared upside down. Gooseflesh abruptly infested his arms and he gunned the engine, spitting gravel from his tires, suddenly desperate to be away from this place. As he drove southwest on Route 3 toward Saranac Lake, he felt chilled to the bone despite the booze burning in his guts.

CHAPTER 2

SINS OF THE FATHER

It was a ten-mile drive to Saranac Lake and by the time Jack stopped at the intersection by the burned down Chinese restaurant that had once featured the best General Tso's chicken in the Adirondacks, the internal chill had pretty much faded away and been replaced by a faint sense of hope. It was an unfamiliar sensation, one he hadn't felt in years. But tomorrow he got his son back and had a plan in place to at least start the reconnection process. It wouldn't be easy—he suffered no delusions that it would be—but it was better than the *drink-*

sleep-repeat pattern that had been his existence the last few years.

He took a left onto Main Street and parked in the small lot at the far end that had once been a gas station, directly across from the Town Hall. This being the weekend, the parking lot was only half full; during the work week, you had a better chance of finding naked pictures of the Pope on Instagram than you did finding a spot in the village's primary parking lots. For being a small, quaint mountain town, Saranac Lake was busier than most people expected.

He locked the Jeep and strolled leisurely up the sidewalk, passing a variety of shops and businesses, waving every now and then when he saw someone he knew. He spotted Wanda, the bank manager who had helped him and Trisha set up their accounts when they first moved to the area, coming out of the furniture store. On the other side of street, Mark, the owner of Ampersound, the local music emporium, was outside washing his storefront window and Jack felt a twinge of guilt that he had converted to digital music last year and stopped buying CDs.

Further up was what natives referred to as the "good" Chinese restaurant and as he passed by, Jack saw Tyler Cunningham inside, grabbing some greasy takeout. Jack didn't stop to talk to Tyler; the man was a bit of an oddball with an assortment of quirks and kinks instead of normal social skills. And his smiles just never seemed quite right.

Jack passed the small Sears outlet, novelty shops, insurance agencies, a tattoo parlor, and the Downhill Bar & Grill, recently transplanted from Lake Placid. He made a mental note to stop after his errand to grab some lunch to go—their Ranch Roast Beef sandwich was to die for.

Just past the restaurant, he arrived at his destination: Big Bad Bill's Sporting Goods. The sign dangling from rusty chains above the sidewalk was so dirty and worn that several letters were missing, so the sign actually read BI BAD ILL S S ORTI G GO DS. It looked like a giant cryptogram or a puzzle on *Wheel of Fortune.*

When Jack walked into Bill's, the first thing he noticed was guns. Row after row of rifles, shotguns, pistols, and even archery equipment and other assorted hunting gear. The place had been here forever and suffered a reputation as a hole in the wall, but there was no denying it was well-stocked and besides, it was the only game in town for firearms unless you felt like driving fifty miles to the Gander Mountain in Plattsburgh. Jack preferred to support local vendors whenever he could rather than toss his cash at fat-cat corporations. Besides, there was just something appealing about Big Bad Bill's. He felt like a kid in a candy shop.

More like an alcoholic at a Jim Beam distillery.

Jack ignored the nasty voice in his head as the owner appeared from a back room. Despite referring to himself as "big" in his store's name, Bill was actually an average sized man, though he did seem to possess a wiry strength; you could actually see cords of lean muscle beneath his skin. He had one of those faces that didn't forecast his age, making it impossible to judge if he was closer to fifty or a hundred.

"Hey, Jack, how's it hangin'? Wait, don't tell me—down an' to the left." He grinned crookedly. It was the same jokey greeting he used on Jack every time he came into the store. Personally, Jack thought it was getting a little old after all these years, but Bill apparently disagreed. "So what brings you down to my humble little rat-hole on a Sunday afternoon?"

"Need a new deer gun," said Jack.

"I've got plenty." Bill gestured around the store. "Rifles, shotguns, handguns, muzzle loaders—hell, I've even got some crossbows. What exactly are ya lookin' for?"

"I don't know … what do you suggest?"

"I suggest wiping your ass front to back before askin' a gal to lick your balls."

Jack blinked at him, not exactly sure what to say to that. "Um, what do you suggest for a deer rifle, I meant."

"Oh. My bad." Bill's eyes twinkled merrily, clearly amused by his own unique brand of humor. "Well, that depends on what kind of huntin' you're doing."

"Uh, deer. Like I said."

Bill rolled his eyes. "Yeah, I got that. Whatta ya think I am, the north end of a southbound donkey? What I meant was, what kind of country you hunting in, what's the terrain like?"

"Oh, sorry. Going up to Scar Lake."

"Scar Lake, hey?" Bill suddenly looked pensive, his brow furrowing in thought. "Well, lemme tell ya, Jack, Scar Lake ain't exactly the friendliest place the Good Lord ever spoke into existence. Lots of big-ass rocks and bad-ass bush and bitch-ass thorns. In other words, nasty shit. Most any shot you get at a buck is gonna be up close an' personal, probably less'n seventy yards, would be my guess, so ya really don't need a high-power rifle. Shotgun would work best in that area and I got just the thing."

He turned, grabbed a shotgun off the rack behind him, and handed it to Jack while rattling off the particulars. "Stoeger Model 2000, semi-automatic, twelve-gauge, synthetic stock, rifled slug barrel. Shorter than a lot of other shotguns and weighs less'n seven pounds. Perfect for crawling around in that nasty bush up around Scar Lake."

Jack had to admit, it sounded like just what he was looking for. He hefted it in his hands and tried to catch a discreet peek at the price tag dangling from a string tied to the trigger guard. But no matter which way he turned the gun, the little white tag twisted away from him. After several seconds, Jack stopped trying to be discreet and just clumsily grabbed the tag to hold it still. He studied the price, then raised an eyebrow at Bill. "Are you serious?"

"I can sell you a more expensive one if ya want," he said with a grin that displayed strong, sturdy teeth stacked in his gums like tombstones.

"No, this is good. Thanks."

Bill chuckled. "Thought you'd say that." They wandered over to the cash register tucked into the corner of the cramped store.

Jack handed over his credit card and listened to Bill whistle tunelessly while waiting for the receipt to print. A few moments later, Bill handed him the receipt along with a complimentary box of slugs and a final warning. "Be careful up there. Scar Lake is dangerous country if you let down your guard."

Jack pocketed the receipt, slung the gun over his shoulder, and said, "Don't worry, careful is my middle name."

"Yeah, well, mine's Cornelius." Bill gave him a faux menacing glare. "Tell anyone and I swear they'll never find your fuckin' corpse."

CHAPTER 3

HE SAW A SPIDER WOMAN

That Sunday evening as the sun begin to sink and impale itself on the pointed peaks of the Adirondack mountains, deep in the darkest, most remote corner of the Scar Lake region, a woman sat Indian-style, hands cupped in front of her. She had been pretty once, and maybe still was—she hadn't seen a mirror in a very long time. But even without a mirror, she knew that any prettiness that might remain was buried beneath the dirt and filth and abuse. Like a sapphire covered in dung.

Her home—well, prison, actually, but her

captors insisted she refer to the place as home—was a ramshackle cabin that was little more than a large, dilapidated shed. She was taken outside once a month to bathe in the icy stream nearby, so she knew that the cabin squatted in a small hollow ringed by massive boulders and that bones carpeted the ground— some animal, but mostly human. Half-buried skulls with ghastly head fractures grinned out from the dirt, black socket holes brimming with blind worms and brutal secrets.

On the south side of the cabin, her captors had erected a makeshift lean-to which looked like it would collapse under the weight of the snow every winter but for some reason never did. It stored a variety of junk, mostly heavy logging chains and hopelessly twisted coils of ancient barbed wire coated in rust.

In the clearing in front of the cabin towered a wooden cross, roughly hewn from heavy logs, the axe-marks clearly visible where steel had chopped into timber. The slap-dash construction of the cross didn't detract from its deadly purpose, however; a skeletal corpse drooped from the beam like a Halloween prop, held in place by rusty railroad spikes impaling the wrists and ankles. Just enough ragged, rancid meat polluted the bones to swell with the stink of death. Had the woman been looking out the window, she would have seen a crow perched almost majestically on the cue-balled skull, claws digging into bone fissures for purchase. Then perhaps she would have turned away in disgust as the crow leaned over and darted its beak into the eye socket and wrenched out a fat, bloated white maggot. Feast secured, the crow took flight into the evening sky, a dark-winged shadow momentarily scarring the orange face of the setting sun.

Inside the cabin, the woman stared at the walls around her. They had been her only view for so long, she knew every inch of them like the back of her hand. They were black and riddled with rot, the floor filthier than a slaughterhouse in a third world country. An apt comparison, given the horrific things she had seen. A large cauldron-like kettle brewed and bubbled on the stove, looking like it should be surrounded by a coven of cackling witches. Actually, the woman would have preferred wicked witches to the savage beasts that actually owned the kettle. She had always believed there were different degrees of evil, but this place had proved it to her. One large table, fashioned from rough-chopped logs like the cross outside and stained a rust-brown color, dominated the center of the squalid room.

The woman had never sat at the table. Her "room" was a padlocked dog kennel, eight feet long, five feet wide, six feet tall, lined with dirty straw that reeked of urine and excrement. She ate here, slept here, voided her bowels here, and sometimes was abused here ... though other times they took her out of the cage to torment her. The abuse was almost always based on the infliction of pain; hence the patchwork of scars all over her body.

She had never been raped in the most basic sense of the word—a fact that still shocked her—though they did occasionally grope her and force her to touch them sexually. Their cocks were large and lumpy, as if the skin was filled with marbles, and while she would never enjoy stroking them to climax, better in her hand than in her mouth. Their sperm was hot and thick and smelled like rotten eggs and she would rather kill herself than have that slime splash the back of her throat.

This was her life now. Imprisoned, caged, trapped in an endless cycle of pain and torment. She looked down into her cupped hands at the monstrously large brown recluse spider sitting calmly in her palm. Disproportionate even to the spider's huge body were the fangs jutting from its mouth. But the woman knew she was in no danger. When you're living in a nightmare, sometimes your friends come in strange forms. "Forever, Mr. Brown," she whispered to her eight-legged companion that looked more like a tarantula than a brown recluse. "That's how long they've kept me in this cage. I don't know how much more I can take…"

Her voice trailed off as she looked down at her arms and legs, a torso that bore more signs of suffering than she could even count. Dressed in only burlap rags that barely covered her, the scars were starkly visible and easy to see, a map of misery carved into her flesh.

She leaned over and raised the spider up to her face, so close that she swore she could see pearls of venom on the oversized fangs. "I know I couldn't have made it this far without you," she said. "You're my eight-legged angel." She almost kissed the spider, but thought better of it. When your best friend is a venomous arachnid, some boundaries are best left uncrossed.

She heard a stick snap outside and shivered.

They were back. Her precious moments of peace were over.

"Hurry, Mr. Brown, they're coming! Go! Go! Go!" Her voice was urgent and the spider responded, darting out of the cage, scuttling across the floor with a speed that no ordinary spider had the right to possess, and then ran up the wall to the blackest corner of the cabin where it settled in the center of its web, waiting and watching.

The cabin door banged open and the woman immediately began to tremble. She lived in hell and now the devils had come home. The leader of the group—the others called him Boss—walked in first. He stood at least 6' 4", maybe taller, his head a festering, misshapen oval of bony knobs and grotesque warts. He glanced at her dispassionately with feral eyes and she glimpsed the predatory intelligence glittering in his gaze. He was the smartest of the pack, capable of actual speech rather than the mere grunts and growls the others relied on to communicate. A sawed-off shotgun was slung across his shoulder, baling twine tied to the abbreviated barrel and grip to form a sling.

Behind him loomed Mongus, a muscle-bound ogre who looked like a massive NFL linebacker afflicted with hyper-acromegaly. His pumpkin-sized head featured beady, soulless eyes on a fat face with unclean folds. Whenever he came close, the woman could see green fungus growing in his facial crevices. He carried a huge, medieval-looking double-bladed axe as easily as most men carry a plastic spoon. She had witnessed him using it enough times to know he kept the edge well-honed.

Cyclops and Junior were the last to enter the cabin. Both of them had to duck under the doorjamb to keep from banging their heads. Cyclops had a bulging blue eye protruding from the left side of his face, but on the right it was just smooth, unbroken skin, without even the hint of a socket. Tucked into his belt was a short-handled, five-pound sledgehammer. It was the only weapon the woman had ever seen him use. The others sometimes mixed and matched weapons, but not Cyclops. If it couldn't be pulverized with the sledge, then he wasn't interested.

Junior lived up to his name. Obviously the youngest of the bunch, but just as hideous as his brethren, if not worse. Though she would never dare give utterance to the thought, the woman figured his IQ was no more than one notch above a turnip.

As if to prove the point, he turned and leered at her with small, stupid eyes that looked like raisins. When he gave her a slobbering grin, his piggish snout and buckteeth sent revulsion and fear pulsing through her in equal measure.

She averted her gaze, looking down at his hands, but that didn't help—his three fingers caressed the handles of the dozen knives tucked in his belt in a suggestive manner that could only be described as demented, dumb-beast sexuality. You didn't have to be a mind-reader to know what he was thinking; the bulge at the front of his pants provided rigid testimony. She wondered what he wanted to stick in her more: his dick or his blades.

I should just kill myself, she thought for the thousandth—maybe millionth—time since her abduction.

But she never did. Never even tried. It wasn't just her belief that suicide was a sin—though that definitely played a part—it was a deep-rooted will to survive. Yes, killing herself would rob these bastards of the thrill of torturing her, but it would also mean they had broken her. She refused to give them that satisfaction.

She hooked her fingers through the metal

links of her cage and watched as Cyclops clomped over to the stove, grabbed the ladle, and stirred the soup pot. It was just water; nothing floated to the top. They hadn't eaten in days. She could sense their growing desperation and it fueled her own fears.

Because desperate men do desperate things.

Cyclops hurled the ladle against the wall, then roared and pointed a sausage-size finger right at her while looking askance at Boss.

Stark terror shot through her. *God, no, please, don't let this happen!*

Boss shook his head, but Cyclops was insistent, his rebellion edged with rage, stomping and grunting and thrusting his finger at her more emphatically. His angry demeanor let Boss know he would not be denied, not this time. Even from her cage, the woman saw fury in Boss' eyes—he did not like being challenged—but he seemed to realize this was a losing fight, so he finally nodded acquiescence. He plucked a leather apron from where it hung on a rusty nail, slipped it on, and then approached the kennel where the woman cowered in fear.

Screaming wouldn't help but she couldn't stop herself. Her cries reverberated off the walls, bouncing back in the form of futile echoes. "No, please! Don't! Please!" Boss ignored her pleas, reached into the cage, grabbed a fistful of her hair, and dragged her out. She struggled as she was wrenched across the floor, but she was no match for Boss' strength. There was nothing she could do but weep and wail as he picked her up and slammed her down on the table. Her spine jarred from the violent impact and pain radiated through her body. But she knew it was nothing compared to the pain about to come.

With the breath knocked out of her, she couldn't even beg for mercy as Mongus held her down while Boss retrieved a chainsaw from the corner of the cabin. It was a big, brutish machine, caked in oil and sawdust ... and blood. When Boss fired it up, it roared like a ravenous demon and spewed exhaust smoke. Tears poured down her face, washing some of the dirt off her face as she prepared herself for horrible agony. She had witnessed others suffer this grisly fate; now it was her turn at the table.

She regained her breath in time to plead, "Why are you doing this to me?" But the throaty rumble of the chainsaw drowned out her voice. Boss slapped the whirring metal teeth against her left arm just below the shoulder. She screamed as flesh and bone dissolved. Blood sprayed the air in a crimson sluice. Her entire body shuddered as the chainsaw chopped off her arm. The pain was beyond anything she could have ever imagined. Cyclops and Junior jumped up and down like kids at a party, laughing obscenely.

Holding the woman down, Mongus was in closer proximity to the blood spray and it rained all over his face in a red splatter. A deformed tongue snaked out of his mouth and licked the gore from his lips. He turned his head to the side and spat out a bone chip.

Through a blurry haze of shock, the woman felt the chainsaw finish cleaving off her arm. Cyclops scurried forward, snatched up the limb, and tossed it in the soup pot. Consciousness began to contract, blackness swirling around the edges of her vision, dark tentacles threatening to drag her down into the void. Half-conscious and delirious with pain, she almost giggled when she saw her own hand sticking up over the edge of the kettle, fingers twitching as if to say goodbye.

She began praying. Not because she believed it would help, but because there was nothing else she could do. "The Lord is my shepherd, I shall not want … the Lord is my shepherd, I shall not want … the Lord is my shepherd …" She squeezed her eyes shut for a moment, as if that would help her desperate supplications reach beyond the smoke-stained ceiling rafters.

When she opened them, Boss was leaning over her face with a portable blowtorch in his hand.

"Save your prayers," he growled. "Ain't no God here."

Maybe not, she thought, somehow managing internal coherency despite her flickering consciousness. *But the devil sure is.*

And then all coherent thought evaporated in a hot blaze of renewed agony as Boss turned the scorching flame onto her blood-gushing stump. She screamed as she heard the sound of her own flesh sizzling and smelled the stink of burnt meat as her wound was brutally cauterized.

She could take no more. Her final scream turned into a whisper as the darkness engulfed her in its merciful embrace. She sank down into the black depths where neither pain nor prayers existed.

In the upper corner of the room, Mr. Brown's six eyes were transfixed on the horrific tableau below, wet and glistening in the murky light.

CHAPTER 4

WE'RE A HAPPY FAMILY

A blinding, relentless light pulled Jack from his slumbering stupor and a dream—nightmare—in which he was making love to Trisha, only to find at the peak of their passion that she turned into a decomposing corpse beneath him. The horrific mental imagery dissipated when he cracked open his eyes and then immediately winced as they were lanced by the sunlight stabbing through his bedroom window. He sat up and clutched his pounding head, which was brutally hammering home the fact that he had drunk way too much last night. No surprise there; he had drunk too much almost every night since he lost her. One of his relatives had once asked him if he was seeing a therapist to deal with his grief. He had told them that he was seeing two of them, and their names were Jim Beam and Wild Turkey. His relative had chuckled at the joke, not realizing Jack wasn't joking.

His stomach suddenly revolted. He bolted from his bed and stumbled into the bathroom, barely having time to lift the lid before he puked into the toilet. He slumped to his knees, a drunkard sinner kneeling before his porcelain god and spent several wrenching moments paying penance in vomit. Cold sweat beaded his brow when he thought it was finally over. He thought wrong. Dry heaves turned to wet ones and water that was almost crystal clear gushed from his mouth.

He'd forgotten to eat anything last night, again. When would he ever learn?

"Oh shit," he managed to mumble before his guts rebelled for what felt like the hundredth time, forcing him to huddle over the bowl. His knees were starting to hurt. After spending so many mornings in this position, you would think he would have learned to put a rug or mat in front of the toilet.

When he finished, he managed to pull himself upright and lurched over to the sink where he washed his mouth out—Listerine, the alcoholic's friend—and splashed water on his face. When he looked into the mirror, his red eyes looked back and accused him of self-destruction. It was an accusation that he could not deny. He rubbed a hand over his bleary features and muttered, "Man, you are not a pretty sight." Probably the understatement of the year.

No longer wanting to face his own degeneration in the mirror, he turned to look at the clock radio perched on a nearby shelf. The large numbers were even redder than his eyes and informed him it was 10:42 a.m. It took him a few foggy seconds to realize why that was important, but then his brain kicked into gear. Something close to panic hit him. "Great! Just fucking great. Of all the times to tie one on." He continued to silently berate himself. *Stupid! You're so fucking stupid, Jack.*

He needed a shower, but there was no time. He quickly changed his clothes, brushed his teeth, ran a comb through his hair, and then sprinted to the Jeep.

******

At Brighton Juvenile Detention Center, Kevin Colter slouched on a bench outside the main building. After three years behind the fence, it felt strange being free. The "nice" thing about prison was that you didn't have to think much for yourself. The officers pretty much told you when to eat, when to sleep, when to work, when to relax ... hell, they practically told you when to do everything except take a crap and jerk off. Those particular activities were left up to your own discretion.

He could clearly remember the day he had been brought to the Detention Center, bussed there along with a handful of other so-called delinquents. Guilty of various crimes—his happened to be robbing Norman's General Store—they had all felt like men, but in hindsight they had been nothing but naïve children. Being inside forced you to grow up fast and the meat grinder of the justice system turned soft boys into hard men. It hadn't been pleasant, but now that it was over, Kevin was thankful for the hardening. Still, he wasn't looking forward to what came next. He had missed many things while behind the fence; his father wasn't one of them.

He ran his fingers, knuckles calloused from numerous brawls on the recreation yard, through what little hair still tufted his head—they gave all the juvies a jailbird haircut—and idly wondered what he would look like if he grew it down to his shoulders like some '80s hair-metal rock star. Maybe he would buy a bandana and enter a Bret Michaels lookalike contest.

Thoughts of rock 'n' roll fakery dissipated as the piercing squeal of tires protesting their punishment announced his father's arrival. Jack took the corner way too fast, nearly rolling the Jeep, and screeched to a halt in front of Kevin. A cloud of road dust drifted in the Jeep's wake.

Jack glanced at the dashboard clock. 11:06 a.m. He was late, but not by much. He rolled down the window, gave Kevin a smile, and said, "Ready to go?" It was a stupid question—after three years in prison, of course he was ready to go—but Jack didn't know what else to say. He hadn't spoken to his son in thirty-six months, so conversation was bound to be awkward from time to time. Maybe *all* the time.

Kevin just sat and slouched and stared at his father for several long moments, the distaste on his face unmistakable. Then he straightened up, stretched, grabbed a small duffel bag, and made his way over to the Jeep. Jack was struck by how much he had grown. Beneath the baggy t-shirt, it was pretty obvious that his son was now a well-muscled man. Before Kevin had been sentenced to juvenile detention, Jack would have easily beaten him in a fight. Now the outcome wouldn't be so easy to predict.

But it wasn't a physical confrontation Kevin seemed to want—it was a verbal one.

He climbed into the Jeep and slammed the door much harder than was necessary. Wasting no time on false pleasantries, he growled, "You're late."

Even his voice is huskier, Jack thought as he whipped the Jeep around and shot back out onto Route 86. The tension he felt translated to his foot, which stomped heavy on the gas pedal. When he realized the needle was pegged at a point on the speedometer that no police officer would find acceptable, Jack forced himself to slow down. Judging from Kevin's sullen tone, he was about to have a bad day and catching a speeding ticket would only make it worse.

Careful to keep his voice neutral, Jack said, "Nice to see you too. And I was barely late. I overslept."

"In what, a barrel of booze?" Kevin sneered.

"You smell like shit. How hard are you hitting the bottle these days, dad?"

Jack resisted the urge to turn and glare at him. Instead, he kept his eyes firmly fixed on the road. "I don't 'hit the bottle,' Kevin. I have a social drink now and then, that's it." The lie fell smooth and easy off his tongue.

But he could tell his son wasn't buying the deception. Kevin's stare burned a hole in the side of his head. When another quarter-mile had rolled beneath the Jeep's wheels, Kevin suddenly reached for the glove box.

"No!" Jack said, throwing out an arm to stop him.

Too late. Kevin held up the full flask like a prosecutor triumphantly revealing a damning piece of evidence. "Yeah, pops," he drawled sarcastically, "because every social drinker keeps a flask in the glove box." He shook his head in disgust.

So much for keeping it neutral, Jack thought. Aloud he said, "I'm your father and I don't have to explain myself to you." He hated how defensive the words sounded even to his own ears.

Kevin was silent for several moments, then said, "You're right, you don't have to explain anything." For a moment, Jack actually dared to hope Kevin was calling a truce, but then his son added, "I'd probably drink myself stupid too if I'd killed my wife because I was such a pussy."

The words were designed to hurt … and hurt they did. Jack would have preferred Kevin just whipped out a knife and started slashing him. It would have been less painful.

He was quiet for several miles, distracting his pain by listening to the sounds of the road, the thrum of the tires on blacktop, the rush of the wind, a bluesy Aerosmith rocker crooning low-volume on the radio. Despite Kevin's presence just an arm's reach away, he felt isolated and alone.

Up ahead a road sign appeared that read "Welcome to Vesper Falls!" It had once simply said "Vesper Falls," but the town board had voted to purchase a bigger, fancier sign and add the "Welcome to" and the exclamation point. Jack figured you could add a thousand exclamation points and it wouldn't make Vesper Falls any more exciting.

As the sign flashed by on the right, he said, "I've made peace with what happened to your mother."

Kevin shook the flask. The booze sloshing around inside sounded like the devil's accusation. "Yeah, I can see that you are really at peace." Scorn roughened his voice.

Keeping his left hand on the steering wheel, Jack reached out with his right to snatch the flask out of Kevin's hand.

"Hey, what the hell?"

Jack rolled down his window and threw out the flask. Glancing in his rearview mirror, he saw it tumble to a stop at the foot of a sign that announced "You Are Now Leaving Vesper Falls." No exclamation points and this sign was much smaller and more simplistic than the one at the other end of town.

"Really?" Kevin said. "What the hell was that all about?"

Something I should have done a long time ago. "I'm done drinking," Jack said. He tried to ignore the panic shredding his guts at the sobering thought of having to spend several days in the woods with his angry, distant son without any alcohol to help him get through.

"Just like that?" Kevin asked.

"Just like that."

Kevin's laugh was tauntingly sarcastic. "Bullshit … but whatever. Now, care to tell me where the hell we're going?"

Jack was grateful for the change of subject. "Scar Lake," he said.

"That shithole? What are we going there for?"

"To get away. Do a little deer hunting. Thought you might like to celebrate your release by putting a bullet in a whitetail."

"I've been locked up and haven't seen a girl for three years, other than prison staff," Kevin said. "So yeah, I'd like to put something in some white tail, if you know what I mean."

Jack shot him a wry glance. "It's deer camp, not a brothel."

"Deer camp." Kevin spat the words as if they left a bad taste in his mouth. "What a stupid idea. In case your observational skills have been compromised by that supposedly final bender you went on last night, the only clothes I have with me are the ones I'm wearing. So if you want to go traipsing through the ass end of God's backyard in pursuit of the elusive whitetail, I'm going to need more appropriate attire." His voice dripped with sarcasm as he added, "Oh yeah, and a gun."

Jack jerked a thumb toward the rear of the Jeep. "I packed you a bag," he said. "And that long box back there is for you."

Kevin glanced over his shoulder. "What's in it?"

"Open it and see."

Kevin reached behind him and pulled the box into the front seat. The length made it awkward, but he managed. He opened the box to find the Stoeger shotgun inside. The masculine scents of gunmetal and cleaning oil filled the Jeep with their testosteronic aroma.

"Got it from Big Bad Bill," Jack said. "Brand new, never been shot. Figured if we had to rely on your good looks to charm the deer into the freezer, we'd go hungry."

He hoped his son's abrasive, resentful shell would crack, at least a little bit, but no such luck. "A Stoeger?" Kevin said mockingly. "Isn't that like the Wal-Mart of shotguns? What's the matter, dad, spend too much money on booze so you couldn't afford a real gun like a Winchester or Remington?"

Kevin's tone abruptly shifted from mocking to venomous. "I can see right through your little plan, *dad*." He sneered the endearment into a twisted obscenity. "You thought giving me this shotgun would patch things up between us, make things all right, bridge the gap, heal the wound, that sort of crap." The lines on his face were hard and rigid, the muscles tight and tense. "But let me tell you something, it's gonna take a whole lot more than a new gun to make me forgive you for what you did to mom."

The words stabbed into Jack's heart. He turned his head to the left, not wanting Kevin to see that his eyes had welled up. Hot shame and equally hot rage seesawed through him at the same time and he blinked back tears as he white-knuckled the steering wheel and struggled to gain control of his wavering emotions.

When he could speak again, Jack said, "I know I failed you, Kevin. I failed all of us. Your mom most of all. But I'm not the same person I was back then." He had a hard time forcing the words out around the lump in his throat.

"Right," said Kevin mercilessly. "Before you were just a coward. Now you're a drunk coward. I guess that's an evolution." He snorted dismissively. "Save your words, dad. They're just as cheap as this shotgun you bought me."

Jack could take no more and lapsed into silence, keeping his eyes on the road as his embers of hope for a fresh start with his son were extinguished by Kevin's cold anger. Not that he could blame him. Kevin had every right to hate his father. Hell, he hated himself most of the time.

Jack glanced at his reflection in the rearview mirror. His face looked older, more wrinkled, than it had an hour ago, and sadness veiled his eyes. He struggled to fight back the internal darkness that wanted to descend. He could not give in. He *would* not give in. He would not give up on his son.

But refusing to acknowledge defeat and knowing what to say to achieve victory is not the same thing, so the embargo of silence remained firmly in place for the rest of the trip. Kevin would not give an inch and Jack felt like he had no more inches to give.

They stopped at the convenience store in Redford to grab some snacks—Jack lingered longingly in front of the beer cooler, but managed to pull himself away—before continuing down the highway, each of them with a Slim Jim protruding from their mouth. They eventually turned off State Route 3 onto side roads that devolved into gravel roads that devolved into dirt roads. Finally, over two hours after leaving the Detention Center, Jack pulled the Jeep into a small parking lot and killed the engine. There were only two other vehicles in the lot—a Ford F150 with New York vanity plates that read "Rickson," and a Chevy Blazer with New Jersey tags. The Blazer had a sticker on the rear window that proclaimed in thick bold letters, MEAT IS MURDER.

Jack shook his head. "Vegans. I'll bet you ten bucks the stinking hypocrites are wearing leather boots while they hike."

He took the key out of the ignition and exited the vehicle. He stretched to relieve the aches of the road, muscles murmuring in relief. He breathed in the mountain air and felt his spirits start to revive, pushing back some of the darkness that had settled over him. He hoped the beautifully rugged surroundings were having a similar effect on Kevin. He turned and looked at his son as he climbed out of the Jeep.

Kevin slowly and deliberately made a point of looking in all directions, not missing a single compass point, then said, "I don't see any lodge."

Jack walked to the back of the Jeep and began grabbing their gear. "It's back a ways. About three miles."

"Three miles!" Kevin sounded as if he had just been told they were walking to Argentina. "Are you shitting me?"

Grinning, Jack tossed a pack to Kevin. "I shit you not. Ice up, son."

"Did you just quote Steve Smith?" Kevin

asked with something close to an amused smile on his face as he slipped his arms through the pack's shoulder straps.

Happy to see something other than sullen bitterness from his son, Jack walked over to a sign-in station next to a large pine tree at the head of the trail. As he jotted their names down on the ledger, he saw that the Ricksons had already checked in. The only other names listed were Vicky and Wayne Parker, presumably the same people who equated eating a hamburger to homicide.

As he shifted his pack to better distribute the weight, Kevin looked at the Blazer's out-of-state tags and shook his head. "What kind of morons drive all the way from New Jersey to come to this godforsaken backcountry?"

"I don't know if they're morons, but their names are Vicky and Wayne Parker," said Jack.

"Morons or not, they should have stuck to safer turf," said Kevin. "This far back in the ass-crack of nowhere, there are at least fifty ways to die and none of them are pleasant."

Jack shrugged. "Hey, they're from Jersey … how smart can they be? Come on, let's get moving."

They followed the narrow trail through the thick forest of pine, maple, birch and oak. The late afternoon sun speared through the foliage in golden shafts. Multicolored leaves cascaded around them, weaving a tapestry of subdued colors before their eyes. Jack thought it was stunningly beautiful, Mother Nature painting on the canvas God created.

A couple hundred yards up the path, they came to a gulch spanned by a makeshift rope-and-log bridge that looked like it might have been constructed right around the end of the Civil War. Jack debated just going down into the gulch, but the sides were steep and jagged boulders protruded from the earthen walls like the discarded teeth of some giant monster. It was just too dangerous.

So is that bridge, his inner voice reminded.

There really was no choice. They either took their chances with the rickety bridge or they turned back, and turning back wasn't an option for Jack. Besides, the Ricksons and Parkers had obviously made it across; if they had not, their busted up bodies would be lying at the bottom of the gulch.

Taking a deep breath, Jack put one tentative foot in front of the other and gingerly crossed the bridge. He only looked down once; seeing the trout stream snaking along the bottom of the gulch far below in liquid-silver flashes made the world spin and he grabbed the thick rope that substituted as a handrail in order to regain his equilibrium. Then he fixed his eyes on the opposite side and finished crossing as quickly as he could. He breathed an audible sigh of relief when his feet touched solid ground again.

He watched anxiously as Kevin trekked across the bridge, but his son seemed to take it all in stride. He even looked down through the gaps in the logs most of the time and showed no signs of vertigo.

That's my boy, Jack thought. *One tough kid.* Aloud he said, "Pretty nerve-wracking, huh?"

Kevin brushed past him with a curt reply. "Only if you're a pussy." He headed into the thick brush alongside the trail. "Be right back. Gotta take a piss."

As he waited for Kevin to answer the call of nature, Jack noticed a pine tree just off the trail with a trunk that forked into a perfect Y about twenty feet up. A vine-covered log had fallen into the crotch and was perfectly balanced, the forked tree acting as the fulcrum to form a giant teeter-totter. The log was angled down, one end disappearing into the thicket while the other end jutted upwards at a forty-five degree angle over the trail.

"Hey," Jack called to Kevin. "Hurry up, will you?"

"I'm coming."

"Really? I thought you were just taking a piss." Jack grinned at his own joke.

"You're hysterical," Kevin said from the bushes.

A salamander caught Jack's eye, scurrying along the trail. He almost missed it, the little lizard's brown and black coloration the perfect camouflage to blend into the dirt and leaves. Jack stepped forward and leaned over for a closer look.

The end of the teeter-totter log that had been jutting out over the trail suddenly dropped down like an executioner's axe, smashing the ground just inches in front of his face and crushing the salamander into amphibious paste. Jack jumped back so quickly that he tripped and landed on his back. His pack cushioned the fall but left him sprawled in the middle of the trail like a turned-over turtle.

Kevin peered at him from behind a thorn bush.

Jack rolled onto his knees and yelled, "You almost killed me!"

Kevin at least had the courtesy to look a little sheepish. "Uh, yeah," he said. "My bad."

Jack climbed to his feet and dusted off his pants while glaring at his son. "You nearly busted my head with a humongous log and all you can say is 'my bad'?"

Kevin reached up and pulled on a vine dangling from the log. The rope-like vegetation was as thick as his forearm. He wrenched it and his end of the log swung down while the opposite end rose back into the air, dripping salamander guts, until it was once again angled above the trail. He then pushed through the brush and rejoined his father on the path.

"Could always be worse," he said, taking the lead as they resumed their hike.

"Yeah? How so?" Jack asked.

Kevin looked back over his shoulder and replied, "I could've said, 'Shit, I missed.'"

Jack frowned at him. "You're not funny."

"Have a drink," Kevin shot back. "Maybe you'll find me more amusing."

A defensive response quickly rose to Jack's lips, but at the last second he decided to let it go. It just wasn't worth it and nothing he said would change Kevin's mind.

They hiked in silence until they came to a sharp bend that led up into a pine grove that was thick with shadows, the sun barely penetrating the twisted, interlocked canopy of needle-laden branches overhead. Kevin halted so abruptly that Jack nearly ran into him.

"Why are you stopping?" he asked.

"Isn't this where…" Kevin's voice trailed off before he finished the question.

Jack finished it for him. "Where Pastor Wainwright's daughter Holly died? Yeah, this is the place."

"I remember reading it in the paper and seeing it on the news. A cougar, right?"

Jack nodded. "Ripped her throat out before Larry even realized what was happening."

"That had to suck."

"Watching someone you love get killed right before your eyes? Yeah, that kind of sucks big time."

Kevin stared at him with piercing eyes. Jack held his gaze for just the briefest of moments and then looked away, letting his son have the moment. He started walking again and even though he didn't really believe in ghosts, he still felt a little strange traipsing over ground where someone had died.

As they walked, he finished the story. "Anyway, Larry went right at the thing with just his walking stick and got busted up pretty bad for it. He had to leave Holly's body behind and go for help. Hurt like he was, it took him almost a whole day—you saw how far we are from the nearest town. By the time anyone got back here, the cougar was long gone and all that was left of Holly was a lot of blood and one finger. It still had her class ring on it." He paused for a moment and shook his head. "I can't even imagine."

"Sure you can," said Kevin.

Now it was Jack's turn to fire off a piercing glare.

Kevin raised his hands in mock surrender. "Just saying."

"How about you don't say another damn word and instead of picking a fight, you pick up the pace," Jack replied. "I'd like to be at the lodge before dark if that's okay with you."

With that, an unspoken truce seemed to be reached and they hiked the final miles without saying another word to each other. By focusing on their pace instead of their hostility, they managed to arrive at the lodge just as the sun was setting. Jack breathed a sigh of relief as the building appeared through the trees. He had not been looking forward to hiking in the dark.

Walking up to the front of the lodge, they stopped and studied it. If Jack was being honest, the place wasn't much to look at. Four walls constructed from rough planks, a tarpaper roof through which poked a leaning-to-the-left chimney chugging smoke, and your basic three-step front porch. Unless the inside looked better than the outside, calling it a lodge was an exercise in wishful thinking. This was a hunter's cabin, pure and simple.

It was obvious that Kevin had taken an instant dislike to the rustic accommodations. The disgust was written on his face as he stared at the outhouse with a half-moon carved in the door, squatting about forty yards away from the cabin on the opposite side of the trail.

"This place doesn't even have plumbing?" he asked in rhetorical disbelief. "Are you kidding me?"

"We're three miles from the nearest road," Jack said, "and that road was eight miles from the nearest town. What did you expect, a Holiday Inn?"

"No, but I didn't expect to play Little House on the Prairie and shit outside either."

"People have been doing their business outside since Adam and Eve, so what's your problem?"

"Spiders," Kevin said matter-of-factly, as if that single word explained everything.

"Spiders?"

"Yeah, spiders," Kevin repeated. "They hide down in the hole and then when you sit down to take a crap, they jump up and bite you on the ass." It was clear from his tone that he was dead serious.

Jack stared at him and then shook his head. "Okay, then. I don't quite know what to say to that, so let's just go meet our roommates."

At that moment, the front door of the cabin flew open and a teenager Jack presumed was Tom Rickson jumped down the steps with a hearty, welcoming smile on his face. It wasn't hard to see why he had gone to rehab for anorexia; Jack had seen more meat on a deer carcass stripped by coyotes. The young man's long—well, compared to Kevin's prison crew-cut, anyway—red hair flopped around his shoulders as he walked up to Jack, hand outstretched, and said, "Hi, I'm Tom. You must be Mr. Colter."

Jack shook Tom's hand. The teenager's grip was weak and fragile, but that was to be expected. "Nice to meet you, Tom," he said. "And call me Jack." He quickly let go of Tom's hand, fearful that he would accidentally crush the bones to powder. Gesturing behind him, he said, "The quiet guy behind me is my son Kevin." He leaned in closer and said in a loud conspiratorial whisper, "He's not quiet all the time, though. At night he snores like a snot-clogged pig."

Tom laughed.

"Real nice, dad." Kevin stepped forward and shook Tom's hand. "Guess it's just us and the geezers for the next few days."

"Looks like it," Tom replied. "But I wouldn't say 'geezer' in front of my dad. He hates that word."

"Speaking of that," Jack said. "Where is your father?"

Before Tom could answer, the outhouse door squeaked open on rusty hinges and a man emerged, tightening his belt. He had the same reddish hair and a neatly cropped beard, with lumberjack arms and a stout chest. If Tom Rickson was the definition of frailty, then his father was the epitome of masculine strength. When he saw the group, his face split into a grin that was a mirror image of his son. He strode up to them and announced in a loud, booming voice, "I highly recommend you let that air out for a while, guys." He waved toward the outhouse. "I'd shake your hands but I should probably wash them first." His eyes sparkled with a good-natured twinkle. "By the way, I'm Paul Rickson, and I see you've met my boy Tom. You must be the Colters."

Jack found himself taking an instant liking to the man. Sometimes you just know good people when you meet them. "We sure are," he said. "I'm Jack and that's my son Kevin. Hope we're not intruding."

Paul gave him a friendly slap on the back. Clearly the man did not know his own strength; Jack felt like his spine had just been slapped out his sternum. "Not at all, my friend, not at all," said Paul. "Come on in, get your gear stowed, and then maybe we can get a big ol' bonfire going, burn some hotdogs, drink some whiskey, and get acquainted."

At the mention of alcohol, Jack felt the craving kick in and swallowed hard. As Paul and Tom led the way up the steps and into the cabin, Jack glanced at Kevin. His son was staring at him and Jack knew that he was thinking, *What are you gonna do, dad?*

Jack didn't have an answer. When the whiskey broke out, he knew what he would want to do, but whether he did it or not remained to be seen. One thing he knew for sure—Kevin already considered him a failure and breaking his promise to stop drinking would just further nail that belief in place.

As they filed into the cabin, nobody glanced toward the outhouse, but even if they had, it was unlikely they would have seen the one-eyed freak concealed in the brush behind the shitter. Cyclops remained silent and still, conditioned for the hunt, the grace of a predator merged with the power of a brute. He didn't even blink when a blowfly crawled across his bulging eye.

He watched in utter stillness for several more minutes, slime and slobber drooling from the corners of his mouth, then slunk away to tell the others.

Father would be pleased.

CHAPTER 5

PUTTING THE "RED" BACK IN MURDERED

Sitting in her kennel, the woman looked at the charred, blackened stump where her arm used to be and fought back the despondency trying so desperately to claim her. It would be easy, so easy, to just give up and surrender to the depths of insanity that clutched at her. She knew there would be peace in letting her mind break. Just stop fighting, let her soul tumble until it shattered like an eggshell against the harsh, hopeless reality that was her existence.

But she couldn't do it. That wasn't who she

was. She was a fighter and not even the loss of a limb could change that.

She still wasn't used to the smell of her cooked flesh. It overpowered even the ripe scent of her own body—she was overdue for a trip to the stream—and constantly assaulted her nostrils in an olfactory reminder of the violation she had suffered. If there was a scintilla of grace in what happened to her that night, it was that she remained unconscious while they devoured her flesh. When she awakened in the dog cage, they had been discarding her meat-stripped bones. She had closed her eyes, but not before seeing that every bone had been snapped in half and the marrow sucked out.

She looked out the window and saw a bloated harvest moon hanging in the heavens. She found solace in the lunar light streaming into her prison, but the night sky was thick with clouds and she knew they would soon snuff out the moonbeams. But that was her life now; slivered moments of peace and respite in the middle of a living hell. She had learned to savor those moments when they came, however brief they might be.

Mr. Brown was crouched on the floor of her cage, keeping her company, but seemed distracted by a moth caught in the web over in the corner, powdery wings beating themselves to pieces against the silken strands as the insect struggled to break free. Still, when she spoke, the spider shuffled its eight feet to turn toward her, letting her know it was listening. "I don't know how much more I can take, Mr. Brown," she said to her companion. "It feels like God has left me here to die."

The spider swung around to glance at the trapped moth, then returned its full attention to the woman.

She gave the arachnid a weak smile. "You don't talk much, do you? But you're a great listener."

She didn't know if the spider actually smiled back or she just imagined it, but either way, she was grateful for the grin.

Both their smiles faded when, from outside the cabin, they heard a woman's shrill, piercing, horrified scream cut through the night.

The door banged open and Mongus stomped in. The warped floorboards rattled beneath his heavy feet. The woman shooed Mr. Brown to safety and the spider darted from the kennel, heading for its web as fast as its eight legs could carry it. Mongus was dragging a middle-aged woman behind him. The woman's head bounced painfully over the threshold. Her "I Love NJ" shirt was torn, tattered, and smeared with blood. Through the rips in the fabric, the woman in the cage glimpsed blood-weeping scratches on the other woman's breasts and realized she had been molested and mauled by the mutants' ragged, dirty, claw-like fingernails.

Boss entered next, one end of a logging chain over his shoulder, the other end wrapped around the ankles of a man. The man's face was caked in blood and his head scraped over the rough wooden floor as Boss dragged him inside the cabin. The man looked at the woman through a mask of red and weakly whispered, "Vicky…"

Vicky screamed, "Wayne!" but then Mongus' fist plowed into her gut so hard that her spleen probably flattened against her spine. The blow literally lifted her off the floor … the floor on which she fell a moment later and curled up in a vomiting ball.

Boss punched Wayne in the face and teeth exploded from his pulped mouth in a shrapnel-spray of shattered enamel. A second blow splattered Wayne's nose from cheek to cheek. Boss then flung the man into the corner like unwanted trash before helping Mongus lift Vicky off the floor. They slammed her down on the table and the woman in the cage winced, knowing whatever came next would be ugly and brutal.

The brutality began when Boss and Mongus each pulled out a blade and started carving on Vicky's head. The sound of the knives slicing through skin was soft and moist. Vicky's shrieks filled the cabin with hopelessness as blood spattered out onto the table and across the arms of the cannibals as they went about their grisly work. The woman in the cage knew there was no real reason for the scalping; it was just something the mutants did sometimes, torture for torture's sake. They had done it plenty of times before and no doubt would do it plenty of times again.

After several agony-filled moments, Mongus peeled off Vicky's scalp like someone tearing the skin off a grape, the sound wet and ripping. Vicky screamed as blood from her mutilated skull streamed down her face. Mongus held the skin-cap in the air like a trophy, ragged strips of tissue and mangled hair gleaming in the moonlight.

Boss walked over to the kennel. The woman hurriedly retreated to the rear as he unlocked the padlock. Mongus unceremoniously dumped Vicky into the cage—they weren't done with her, not by a long shot—and Boss locked it back up.

The two women stared at each other. One with eyes sad and haunted from years in hell. One with eyes bewildered and terrified because her hell had just begun.

Up in the corner, Mr. Brown kept one of its three pairs of eyes on the scene below while it slowly stalked over to the moth entangled in the web. The insect's frantic struggles had considerably weakened and the spider hovered over its prey, patiently waiting for just the right moment to strike.

Boss yanked Wayne to his feet. The New Jersey native was a relatively fit man and tried to fight back, but his strength was nothing compared to Boss' brute power. The leader of the cannibal pack smashed two brain-blasting blows to Wayne's jaw that knocked him three-quarters of the way toward unconsciousness. The woman in the cage knew Boss had pulled his punches; if he had struck Wayne full force, he would have caved in the man's skull like an eggshell. She had seen him do it more times than she cared to count.

Boss stretched Wayne out on the torture

table, still slick with his wife's blood, and all four of the flesh-eating mutants surrounded him, each bearing a sharp-edged instrument of some sort. They raised the blades over their head. Wayne had one second to cry out in a slurred, semi-conscious voice, "No!" And then all four weapons exploded down into his body. The *thunk-thunk-thunk-thunk* of steel punching into flesh echoed off the walls of the cabin, savage music with a grisly rhythm.

Mr. Brown had seen it all before and didn't need to see it again. The spider turned away and sank its oversized fangs into the moth, driving deadly needles into the soft body to feed.

******

The bonfire burned high and bright, flames leaping off the logs and casting flickering shadows into the intertwined canopy of pine boughs overhead. Jack and Paul sat side by side in camp chairs on one side of the fire while their sons sat on the other. Tom was showing Kevin the intricacies of a Nintendo 2DS. They didn't allow many electronics in lockup, so Kevin was unfamiliar with the gaming system. But apparently he was catching on quick, because Tom yelped, "Holy crap, dude, you're a natural! You came within five thousand points of beating my high score!"

Jack squashed a melting marshmallow between two graham crackers and took a bite. He suddenly realized he had forgotten the chocolate, but decided he didn't really care. "Oh, man, that's good," he said appreciatively. "If I get to Heaven and find out they don't serve S'mores, I'm asking to go somewhere else." He reached over, tapped Paul on the shoulder, and pointed to their sons. "Can you believe we bring them all the way out here to God's country and all they want to do is play videogames?"

Paul broke off a piece of Hershey's bar. After Jack had pulled him aside and explained the alcohol situation, he had readily agreed to skip the whiskey, but he had compensated by stuffing himself with half a dozen S'mores. Now he was forgoing the graham crackers and marshmallow and just nibbling on the chocolate. His face was solemn and thoughtful in the firelight as he replied, "I'm just happy Tom's here at all. I almost lost him. If you think he's skinny now … well, skinny doesn't even begin to describe what he looked like before rehab."

Jack nodded as if he understood, but looking across the fire at Tom, it was hard to imagine him much skinnier. He must have been nearly cadaverous before hitting rehab. "He doesn't seem too bent out of shape about it," Jack remarked.

"He was at first," Paul replied. "Our relationship went through a pretty rough patch."

"I can relate," Jack said. "Kevin and I are still going through a rough patch." The S'more seemed to abruptly lose its flavor and Jack tossed it in the fire. The marshmallow melted and ran in sticky white rivulets that sizzled in the flames.

"Yeah, I heard," Paul said. "Small town like Vesper Falls, it's hard not to hear the rattling of skeletons in people's closets."

Jack winced. For some reason, the word "skeleton" made him think of Tricia, lying six feet underground, no doubt nothing but bones by now. He stared into the fire, shadows dancing over his face, as a single tear slid down his cheek. He turned his head to hide his shame.

Paul continued, "I know you've heard this a million times, Jack, but you didn't kill your wife. *He* killed her. The man in the ski mask.

That wasn't you." His voice was warm and compassionate.

"I was scared so I let her die," Jack said quietly, brushing away the tear. "I was a coward. There's no other way to put it. I know it. Kevin knows it. And he'll never forgive me. Not without a miracle."

Paul reached over and put a comforting hand on Jack's shoulder before standing up and saying, "Well, a miracle is what it's gonna take for us to get out of bed at the crack of dawn if we don't get some shut eye." Turning to Tom and Kevin, he said, "C'mon, guys, let's put the games away and hit the sack. The deer get up early and so do we."

******

Jack awoke a few minutes before the alarm was set to blare at 4:45 a.m. He allowed his eyes to adjust to the lack of light as he listened to Kevin, Tom, and Paul snoring away in their sleeping bags, dreams of big bucks no doubt frolicking through their heads. He swung his legs over the side of his bunk and peered at the clock. As he did so, he thought he glimpsed something move quick and furtive outside the small octagonal window above the dresser. He padded over in his bare feet to peer outside.

The glass was fogged over and he reached up to wipe it off. But the moisture wasn't on the inside of the pane, it was on the outside.

Like someone or something had been breathing on it.

Jack looked outside, but it was too dark to see much. He could barely make out the nearest trees and they were less than five yards away. From the outside, the window was seven feet off the ground. Jack stared at the slowly dissipating patch of fog on the glass again.

A bear? Or maybe a Sasquatch?

He grinned at the thought. He had heard reports of Sasquatch sightings to the south, down in the Ticonderoga and Dresden areas, but never this far north. He wasn't sure he believed in the existence of such creatures, but he did wonder from time to time what he would do if he encountered one. Crap his pants, was the most likely answer.

The buzz of the alarm interrupted his thoughts. He stopped thinking about the fogged up window and started thinking about putting a big buck in his crosshairs. He slapped his hand down on the alarm clock to silence it. He heard the rest of the guys squirming in their bunks, assorted moans and groans filling the room as they went through the waking up process.

"Rise an' shine, boys," Jack said in an exaggerated drawl. "Daylight's a-wastin'."

"There's no daylight yet," Kevin countered sleepily.

"Early bird gets the worm," Jack replied. "Early hunter gets the buck."

As Paul climbed out of his bunk, he muttered, "Yeah, but don't forget, the early worm gets eaten."

Jack chuckled and began pulling on his hunting gear.

******

Paul whipped up a big batch of scrambled eggs, venison sausage, and home fries, cooked in enough butter to send cholesterol levels skyrocketing and washed down with black coffee strong enough to grow hair on a concrete block. The combination of greasy food and bitter brew ensured they all made a pre-hunt trip to the outhouse despite Kevin's dire warnings of butt-chomping spiders.

Bellies full and guts purged, they all checked their walkie-talkies to ensure their frequencies were synchronized, then walked up the trail with Paul lecturing about various safety aspects of deer-hunting. His primary point seemed to be that you needed to be positive you were shooting at a whitetail buck and not another hunter hunkered in the brush. "If you're not sure, then don't pull the trigger," he said.

About a hundred and fifty yards past the cabin, the path split in three directions. Jack and Paul continued on the main path that would take them up to the beaver dams. Kevin broke right to follow a brook that snaked its way through the bottom of a gully. Tom took the left-hand branch, threading through some beech saplings at the base of a knob (or small mountain; he couldn't tell which it was) until he found himself standing at the edge of a small, stagnant pond populated with dead trees and coated with green gunk. He circled the pond and eventually settled in a copse of oak trees overlooking an overgrown clear-cut that had been logged off years ago and allowed to brush over.

It was ideal habitat for deer, especially a wary trophy buck with a nice crown of bone on its head. Tom wasn't a die-hard hunter—he mostly did it to make his father happy in an attempt to restore their once-broken relationship—but he certainly would not pass up a big rack if one happened to stroll this way.

Dawn was just streaking the sky with grey when he found a stump. Best of all, a thick layer of moss carpeted the top, forming a natural cushion. The frost-coated moss crackled a bit when he sat down, but he couldn't feel the coldness through his thermal underwear and insulated hunting pants.

His breath plumed in the crisp autumn air as he leaned his shotgun against a nearby tree. In a violation of basic firearms protocol, he clicked off the safety so that if a buck appeared and he had to quickly reach for the gun, he wouldn't waste time fumbling around with the safety. He would just be able to grab the gun and shoot. *Besides,* he justified to himself, *there's nobody else around, so even if the gun accidentally goes off, nobody will get hurt.*

Comfortable and satisfied with his setup, Tom pulled out his Nintendo 2DS. He muted the volume to avoid alerting any deer in the area to his presence, then began playing the latest *Grand Theft Auto*. He chuckled to himself as his thumbs flew over the controls. Times sure had changed. Hard to believe in the old days hunters had to bring a paperback with them to kill time while on watch.

Immersed in the game, he never sensed the danger that suddenly loomed before him. Never felt the large shadow that suddenly enveloped him. Never realized he was in the final moments of his about-to-be-cut-short life. Just before he died, he heard a twig snap in front of him. He pulled himself out of virtual reality and back into the real world just in time to see a huge axe arcing down at his head.

It happened so fast that there was no time for fear to register. His reaction was instant and instinctive.

He raised his hand.

The blade of the axe struck him between the middle and ring finger, carved through his palm, and split his arm open all the way to the elbow. Blood spurted onto the frosty ground and brutalized bone shards jutted from ruptured flesh.

Shocked, Tom didn't even feel any pain. He didn't scream. He just stared at his wounded arm, cut in two like a piece of firewood.

Mongus brought the axe back around and with an animalist grunt planted the blade in the top of Tom's head. It was a perfectly delivered killing stroke.

The axe made a loud, wet crunching sound as the blade bit through skull-bone until it was buried in the boy's neck. Crimson gore geysered as Tom's face cracked apart, both eyes crossed as if trying to find each other. Brain matter curdled out of his smashed head like spoiled cottage cheese as the corpse twitched in a spastic death dance.

Mongus yanked his axe free and the body fell to the ground. Blood immediately formed a halo around the shattered skull, melting the frost with its grisly heat. Boss, Cyclops, and Junior emerged from the woods to examine the kill.

Boss reached down with a brawny fist, grabbed the front of Tom's hunting jacket, and hoisted the corpse into the air. He looked at it the way a fisherman looks at a freshly-caught trout to determine if it's worth keeping or not. He shook the body to get a feel for its weight, paying no mind as the remaining brains slopped out of the crushed cranium and splatted on the ground. When he realized the featherweight remains of Tom Rickson wouldn't make a snack, let alone a meal, he growled, "Leave him. Ain't nothing but gristle," and then disgustedly tossed the corpse aside like an unwanted rag doll.

The body tumbled over the crunchy leaves until it crashed into the tree the shotgun was leaning against. The axe-chopped arm flopped against the gun, knocking it over. It struck the ground and since the safety wasn't engaged, the jarring impact triggered a shot.

The boom thundered through the woods.

******

Jack and Paul had just split up to head to separate hunting spots when the shotgun blast shattered the dawn air. They quickly reconvened with each other and Jack pointed to the southeast. "Sounds like it came from over there," he said. The trail for the last several hundred yards had gradually steepened and he was panting a bit from the exertion. Nothing like a good hike to make you realize you're no longer in prime physical condition.

"That's where Tom is," Paul said excitedly. "Hope he nailed a big one." He grinned proudly and slapped Jack on the shoulder with a gloved hand. "You know what they say: one shot, one kill. Bet you dollars to dimes something just bought the farm."

"Sorry, I'm saving my money for tonight's poker game," Jack said. "Now let's go see if he needs help with the gutting."

******

Like Tom, Kevin had located a mossy stump on which to sit. The location was a hardwood ridge, the forest floor practically rolling with acorns of both the red oak and white oak variety. Kevin knew acorns were one of deer's favorite foods, a fact proven by the countless piles of pebbled scat. He also spotted several tree rubs where bucks had scraped their antlers against sapling trunks to clean the velvet off the bone. All in all, more than enough sign to justify setting up watch in the hopes of ambushing an unsuspecting whitetail.

Unlike Tom, he did not have a Nintendo 2DS, so all he had to pass the time with were his thoughts. He would have rather had the Nintendo. When he was alone like this, all he could think about was his dead mother, his cowardly father, and the years he had spent behind bars. Oh, sure, dad was trying to make things right, but he was trying too hard … while also not trying hard enough. It would take more than a new shotgun and a hunting trip to heal the wounds between them.

Maybe I should cut him some slack, Kevin thought. *At least he's trying.*

He suddenly slapped the side of his neck. When he pulled his hand back, a splat of blood stained his palm. He also spotted some tiny, twisted legs and crushed wings mixed into the mess. "Stupid mosquitoes," he muttered. Still, he would rather deal with mosquitoes than deer flies. Those things frigging *hurt* when they bit you.

He opened his knapsack, pulled out a paper towel, and began wiping off his hand and neck. He hoped there were no other hunters in the vicinity—unlikely, given their remote location—that might mistake the white paper towel for the tail of a deer and throw a shot in his direction.

He suddenly froze as he heard something crashing through the trees toward him.

The noise was loud, all crackling leaves and snapping twigs and breaking branches. It sounded like a deer on the run, coming his way fast. He grabbed the Stoeger, clicked off the safety, and pointed the barrel in the direction from which the crashing sounds were originating. He looked through the scope, heart hammering, spiked on adrenaline, waiting for the deer to appear. He mentally envisioned making the perfect kill-shot, putting a twelve-gauge slug in a ten-pointer's heart.

Of course, it was more likely just a doe or a

spike-horn.

The noise grew louder and louder … and then completely stopped.

Kevin held still, but his eyes flicked back and forth in their sockets, peering into the woods. He waited for what seemed like several minutes, but was probably more like thirty seconds. Finally, when no deer appeared, he lifted the shotgun to his shoulder and peered through the scope. With the magnification dialed all the way up to 9X, whatever he was looking at through the scope was brought into much closer focus, but it also considerably narrowed his field of vision.

Keeping his eyes glued to the scope, he swung the shotgun slowly to the left, scanning the trees, the rocks, the brush.

Nothing.

No deer.

But I know I heard one. It's got to be around here somewhere.

He swung the shotgun back to the right and a woman's bloody head suddenly filled his crosshairs. One second she wasn't there, the next she was, popping into frame like some kind of gruesome jack-in-the-box. He nearly jumped out of his skin. "Holy shit!" he yelped.

She had no hair on most of her head, just a

filleted scalp covered with matted gore. Dried blood streaked her face into a reddish-brown mask. Kevin lowered the gun as the woman screamed, "Help me! Please help me!"

Kevin stood up and took a step backward, not quite sure what to make of the injured woman in front of him. "Who are you?" he said. "What the hell happened?" There seemed to be no immediate threat, so he slung the shotgun over his shoulder.

The woman stared at him for a moment. She seemed dazed, maybe from blood loss. Then she blinked and rushed toward him.

"Hey, lady, are you okay?" he asked, taking another automatic step back, retreating from the woman's panicked charge.

He didn't move fast enough. The woman closed the gap and her hand shot out to grab his arm, fingers digging desperately into the sleeve of his hunting coat. Kevin tried to pull away, but her grip was too strong. The woman was clearly half out of her mind. "Please!" she said frantically. "Come with me! They're going to kill him! Please, you have to help!"

Kill? Did she just say kill? Kevin tried to take another step back but the woman's other hand reached out and grabbed his arm, holding him in place. "Relax, lady," Kevin said. "You need to take a breath, calm down, and then tell me what the hell is going on. Who's gonna kill you? Go with you where?"

The woman abruptly let go of him. "This way!" she said, hurrying back the way she had just came. Not really a path; more like a game trail.

"Hold on." Kevin reached into his pocket and pulled out a two-way radio. He keyed the mike and said, "Dad, you there?"

He heard a squelch of static and then the woman darted back and slapped the radio out of his hand. He glared at her the as the radio broke into pieces on the rocks at his feet. Pieces of shattered casing and busted circuitry bounced against his boots.

"There's no time for that!" The woman practically screamed the words.

"What the hell is wrong with you?" Kevin snapped.

"There's no time! We have to hurry! They're going to kill him!"

"Maybe I should go get my father first."

"There's no time!"

The woman was starting to sound like a broken record. "All right, I got it, there's no time," Kevin said. "So let's go." He took the shotgun off his shoulder, taking comfort in the fact that there was a shell in the chamber as he followed the scalped woman deeper into the woods.

******

Jack heard Kevin's voice on the radio. *"Dad, you there?"*

He plucked the radio from where it hung from a clip on his belt and raised it to his lips. "Yeah, I'm here." He took his thumb off the transmit button and waited.

Silence.

Jack keyed the mike again. "Hey, Kevin, can you hear me?"

The radio remained mute.

Jack gave the thing a good shake and then tried again. "Kevin, are you there?" When there was still no answer, he turned to Paul. "Something's wrong."

"Not necessarily," said Paul.

"I've got a bad feeling."

"He's your son and I would never tell you not to trust your gut," Paul said. "Tell you what, why don't you go check on him and I'll go find Tom. We can meet back at the lodge."

Jack nodded. "Sounds like a plan." He slapped Paul on the shoulder and then headed back the way they had just come, his feet picking up the pace while a sickening sense of worry settled in the pit of his stomach.

******

Paul watched Jack trot off, hoping that the man was wrong and that Kevin was not in any kind of trouble. When Jack disappeared around a bend in the trail, he shrugged his pack into a more comfortable position and then continued in Tom's direction. He didn't know exactly where his son had chosen to hunt, but he knew the general vicinity. Every fifty yards or so he yelled Tom's name.

He continued to walk and holler until he came to an oak grove near a clear-cut. He paused, cupped both his hands around his mouth, and yelled, "Hey, Tom! Where are you?"

Nobody responded, but he did hear something rustling in the thick tree canopy above him. Probably a squirrel. Where there were deer, there were squirrels, both creatures finding the tasty attraction of the acorns impossible to resist. These early morning hours were prime feeding time for squirrels too. Paul could hear the thing hopping from branch to branch.

"All right, you stupid tree rat," he growled.

"I'm gonna blow your ass into stew meat." He looked up and started to raise his rifle. He would rather have venison steaks for dinner, but some sautéed squirrel would do just fine too.

Something large tumbled from the trees, bouncing and ricocheting off the branches as it fell, heading right for him. Paul jumped to the side, narrowly avoiding being crushed by the object, which crashed to the ground in front of him like a lumpy sack of sand. He flinched as something wet spattered his face...

...and then looked down at his son's dead body.

Tom's head was almost completely split in two, recognizable only because of the red hair. One of the last sights Paul would ever see on this earth was the crimson-coated interior of his son's cranial cavity. He dropped his rifle from fingers suddenly too weak to hold it and fell to his knees, screaming in anguish. The screams seemed to last forever, and when they stopped, the sobbing began. Lost in that grief-stricken moment, Paul Rickson no longer gave a damn if he lived or died.

So he didn't care when a large shadow suddenly loomed over him. The only reason he had to live was now lying in front of him, brutally transformed from repentant son to butchered meat. He didn't even bother to turn around and face the danger behind him. He simply gathered Tom in his arms and wept, anointing him with tears. He would never let his son go.

Not even when Mongus' massive axe shattered his spine like dry kindling.

CHAPTER 6

A JACK OF ALL TRADES

Barren branches reached out and clutched at Kevin like skeletal hands and thorny brush clawed at his clothes as he followed Vicky's hurtling flight down the path. Blood dripped from her scalped head every few yards and stained the earth beneath their running feet. Normally it would have been hard not to stare at her skinned skull, but he was too busy trying not to stumble and break an ankle. The open woods had given way to much more rugged terrain, but Vicky showed no sign of slowing down.

Kevin was really starting to huff and was just about to ask, "How much farther?" when they threaded their way between two huge boulders and burst out of the brush into a small hollow where a cabin stood. It looked exactly like the kind of cabin a mountain hermit would have built back in the 1800s.

Except for the large cross stuck in the ground with a skeleton nailed to it.

And the carpet of bones.

Fear uncoiled in his guts and began a slow-crawl through his system. "What is this place?" he asked. He had been in some tough spots behind the razor wire, but some primal instinct warned him that he had never been as screwed as he was right now.

"I'm sorry, so sorry. They said they would let us go if I brought you here. I'm sorry, so, so sorry." Vicky was babbling and Kevin knew that was never a good sign. "I'm so, so sorry, but I really didn't have a choice."

"What are you talking about?" Kevin demanded. "*Who* are you talking about?"

Vicky pointed over his shoulder. "Him."

Kevin turned just in time to catch Boss' wicked haymaker flush on the jaw. The blow spun him around so fast that the shotgun went sailing in one direction and his knapsack went flying in the other. Both landed unceremoniously in the dirt. A second later, his unconscious body joined them.

******

It took Jack longer than he hoped to find where Kevin had set up watch, but when he saw the shattered walkie-talkie, it confirmed his suspicions that his son was in trouble. Panic hammered at him, but he forced himself to keep it under control. He scanned the woods for any sign of Kevin and soon noticed drops of blood on the ground. Kevin's blood, someone else's blood, deer blood … Jack had no idea and no way to figure it out. He simply started following the red droplets, tracking his son the way he would have tracked a wounded deer, praying like hell that there was still enough time to rescue his son from whatever danger he was in.

******

When Kevin regained consciousness, he found himself staring at the dirt, just inches below him. He was suspended face-down in a spread-eagled position by thick ropes stretched taut between four large wooden poles that pulled his arms and legs in all directions. The agony from his wrenched joints was excruciating. His skull pounded with pain from the blow that had knocked him out. He coughed to clear his dry throat, not factoring in his close proximity to the ground, and a cloud of dirt slapped him in the face.

He strained to lift his head and saw Vicky and another man. During their urgent flight through the woods, Kevin had pieced together from Vicky's babblings that she had been hiking with her husband, Wayne, so he presumed that was who the man was. If so, he was in a rough shape; Junior and Cyclops were holding him upright and he was covered with stab wounds. He looked like he already had one foot in the grave and all it would take was a soft puff from the Reaper to put him in the rest of the way. If not for the mutants supporting his nearly-dead weight, Wayne would have crumbled to the ground, likely never to rise again.

Turning his head slightly, Kevin saw Mongus wrapping rusty strands of barbed wire around an equally rusty ten-foot length of logging chain, threading the metal thorns through the steel links. The sight promised unimaginable pain and did nothing to soothe Kevin's nerves.

"I did what you asked." He heard Vicky's plaintive voice pleading with Boss and turned his head in their direction, neck straining. "I brought him here. So please, let us go, like you promised."

Boss stared at her with a cruel smile that only made his ugly face even uglier. "You want me to let him go?"

Vicky nodded. "Yes, please."

Kevin could tell plain as day what was coming next. Had she not been hanging onto her last strand of desperate hope, Vicky no doubt would have seen it too. But as it was, she never saw it coming.

Boss looked over at Junior and Cyclops and gave them a nod. They let go of Wayne, who immediately dropped to his knees, head lolling weakly forward until his chin touched his chest. In one violent blur of motion, Junior whipped a knife from his belt, jerked Wayne's head back, and gashed his throat open. Not the clean slice of a skilled assassin, but rather the vicious hacking and chopping of an amateur butcher. Kevin could hear the sound of ripping flesh and see the blood gushing from Wayne's sawed open neck.

"NOOOOO!" screamed Vicky. The horrible cry ricocheted off the boulders surrounding the hollow and echoed back at her in a torturous taunt.

Wayne clutched at his savaged throat for a moment, his fingers funneling the spraying blood into jets, and then toppled onto his face. He exhaled his final breath in a wet gurgle as the ground beneath him became crimson mud.

Vicky threw herself at Boss in a grief-stricken rage, pounding her fists against his chest as she screamed, "You bastard! You promised!" But that outburst sapped her last reserves of strength and she slid to the ground, kneeling in front of her captor, arms now hanging limply at her side. "You promised," she whimpered. "You promised you would let us go." She sounded betrayed, as if she had actually believed the mutants would keep their word.

Boss leered at the woman on her knees before him, then grabbed his sawed-off shotgun and shoved it into Vicky's face. He grinned lecherously and growled, "Suck it."

Vicky looked up at him with terrified eyes as Boss pressed the muzzle against her lips, forcing them apart. She whimpered when the cold steel pried open her mouth; those whimpers turned to gags when the steel invaded her throat. Boss rammed the barrel in and out, his finger toying with the trigger with every thrust. Kevin winced every time, fully expecting a shotgun blast to detonate Vicky's head at any second.

She was clearly broken. She just closed her eyes and endured the violation, no fight left in her, just waiting for it to be over. When Boss finally jerked the shotgun all the way out, blood dripped from the muzzle and more blood dribbled from the corners of her mouth. She fell forward, sobbing and coughing and choking. She heaved several times, vomiting bloody bile into the dirt.

She finally stopped and looked up at Boss wearily as if to say, *What next?*

Kevin fully expected the mutant leader to force something else into Vicky's mouth. Orally raping her with the shotgun had clearly aroused him; the bulge at the front of his pants was disturbingly obvious.

But instead, Boss pointed toward the woods beyond the boulders and growled, "Go."

Vicky looked shocked. "You're … you're not going to kill me?"

"Go," Boss repeated, gesturing dismissively.

She slowly climbed to her feet, flinching at every movement, clearly expecting a shotgun blast at any moment. She looked towards the woods and took a hesitant step forward.

Boss' patience was gone. He rammed the shotgun into her chest and gave her a rough shove. "Go!" he roared. "Won't tell you again."

Vicky turned and sprinted blindly into the woods. She didn't know which direction to head, but right now that didn't matter. All that mattered was that against all odds, she was free. Getting away from her captors was not her primary goal—it was her *only* goal. The thick brush blocked her vision and tore at her skin.

Her freedom lasted for a quarter-mile before coming to an abrupt halt. She never saw the bear trap camouflaged beneath a screen of leaves and branches. Running in blind, panicked flight, she set her foot squarely down on the plate. The massive jaws snapped shut just below her knee, the metal teeth easily shearing through flesh and muscle and biting all the way to the bone. She jerked to a stop and screamed in pain.

The scream rose in pitch when she saw two giant logs suspended from ropes swinging down toward her, one on each side. And then the scream died—along with Vicky—as the two logs slammed together, crushing her skull between them.

Mongus appeared a short time later to remove the body from the bear trap. He reached down and pushed the metal jaws the rest of the way through the tibia, severing the leg. He then examined Vicky's head and judged the pulpy mess to not be worth saving, so he cut it off and tossed it aside. It landed in the brush with a soggy splat. Satisfied, he then grabbed Vicky's remaining leg and began dragging the headless corpse back to the cabin.

No point in wasting good food.

******

Jack froze when Vicky's agonized scream reverberated through the forest and winced when it was cut short. No scream ended that abruptly for a good reason. *Thank God it wasn't Kevin,* he thought and then immediately felt guilty for taking solace in someone else's pain. But the guilt didn't change how he felt—he wasn't glad the woman was suffering, but he was glad it wasn't his son.

As the final echoes of the screams began to fade, Jack listened intently, doing his best to pinpoint the direction. Then he began to move again, for once in his life running toward danger instead of away from it. And as he ran, he whispered, "I'm coming, Kevin. I'm coming."

******

Kevin lifted his head and saw Boss smile wickedly as Mongus dragged Vicky's headless, one-legged corpse into the hollow, dumping it by one of the boulders. Kevin didn't want to think about why the pack of mutants wanted the body. He seriously doubted they were saving the corpse in order to give it a proper Christian burial.

He stopped wondering about the fate of Vicky's corpse and started worrying about his own fate when he saw Boss gesture in his direction. Junior walked toward him, plucking a knife from his belt. For some strange reason, Kevin wondered how sharp it was. He suspected he was about to find out.

He struggled against the ropes holding him, his already punished joints screaming in painful protest. "Get the fuck away from me!" he yelled.

Junior ignored Kevin's frantic thrashing and with a few deft strokes, slashed his shirt away from his body, exposing his back to the crisp morning air. Kevin flinched every time he felt the cold steel graze his skin, but Junior possessed deft skill with the blade and the only thing the razored edge sliced was cloth. Kevin's back remained uncut.

For now.

His task finished, Junior moved away.

Kevin fought against his bonds one more time. He knew it was useless, but he couldn't just give up without a fight. He suffered no delusions—whatever was about to happen next would be bad. *Real* bad.

Mongus picked up the logging chain wrapped in barbed wire and Kevin felt his guts turn to water. The heavy chain coiled in the giant's fist like a medieval whip as he stepped behind Kevin. Kevin began to tremble, unable to control his fear, as Mongus prepared to scourge his helpless body. The first blow from the chain would probably shatter his spine … then the barbs would strip the flesh from the broken bone shards.

Mongus raised the chain high as the other watched with savage glee.

Kevin gritted his teeth. *Oh God, let this be over quick.*

The answer to his grim prayer came in the roar of a shotgun blast. Mongus' right hand— the one holding the logging chain—suddenly exploded like an overstuffed sausage. As the echo of the gunshot bounced from boulder to boulder, Mongus stared stupidly at the ragged stump of his wrist as if wondering where the hell his hand went.

Take that, motherfucker, Kevin thought. *Now you see it, now you don't.*

And then he heard his father's voice boom through the hollow.

"Nobody move or I'll kill every one of you!"

Junior apparently didn't believe in obeying orders. He immediately bolted for the cabin's front door. Jack punished his disobedience by putting a slug right between his shoulder blades. It blew through Junior's body and exploded a gaping exit wound in his chest. The slug's walloping impact punched the mutant face-down in the dirt. He went from alive to dead in mere seconds and skidded into hell on a slick of his own blood.

"Anyone else want to try me?" Jack's voice held a hard, ruthless, *don't fuck with me* edge that Kevin had never heard before.

Boss snarled in rage but motioned for Cyclops and Mongus to stay put. "What do you want?" he bellowed.

"My son," Jack replied. "Let him go."

"No." Boss uttered the refusal in a tone that indicated he believed the matter was settled.

Another shotgun blast thundered through

the morning air. The ground exploded less than a foot in front of Boss, peppering his pants with debris. "Let's try this again," Jack said. "I want my son."

Boss moved deceptively fast, his long strides covering a lot of ground in little time, and before Jack could react, the mutant leader had his sawed-off shotgun leveled against Kevin's skull. Surprisingly, Kevin felt no fear at this new development. Better a shotgun blast to the head than be ripped apart by a logging chain wrapped in barbed wire.

"Come down here or I'll blow his head off," Boss warned. Maybe it was just Kevin's precarious position, but he didn't think it sounded like a bluff.

"Then you die next," Jack promised. "All of you."

That didn't sound like a bluff either.

From the corner of his eye, Kevin saw Boss' finger tighten on the trigger as he snarled, "Won't ask again."

Kevin squeezed his eyes shut and waited for the twelve-gauge eruption that would snuff out his young life. When nothing happened, he opened them and saw his father emerging from the thorny thicket and making his way down one of the trails into the hollow. He slowly approached Boss and Kevin, shotgun raised and ready.

"Drop the gun," Boss ordered.

"Let him go," Jack countered.

"Not until you drop the gun."

Jack sighed. "Listen, we can do this dance all day long, but I can promise you that I'm not putting this gun down until I know my son is safe."

"Fine." Boss looked down at Kevin, then locked eyes with Jack once again. "You for him."

Jack's face went pale. "What do you mean?" he asked, but it was obvious from his voice that he knew exactly what the mutant meant.

Boss spelled it out anyway. "Your boy goes. You take his place."

Jack's mind instantly flashbacked with horror to that terrible day. *Trisha gasping ... Kevin sobbing ... the maniacal eyes behind the ski mask ... the gun pressed to Trisha's skull ... the haunting words ... "Whether she lives or dies is entirely up to you. The choice is all yours." ... his cowardly decision that cost Trisha her life...*

Now he had to make that decision all over again as fear froze the blood in his veins. He stared at Boss, knowing what he needed to do, but not knowing if he could.

Kevin said, "Dad … don't."

Boss kicked him in the side to shut him up.

Jack took a step forward, pointing his shotgun at Boss' face. "Don't touch him."

"Somebody's dying," Boss growled. "You or him. Your choice."

"I know," Jack said with all the solemnity that such a life-changing moment deserved. He swallowed hard and made his decision. "Let him go. I'll take his place."

"Drop the gun first."

"Not a chance in hell," Jack said. "Not until I know my son is safe. When I've decided he's far enough away, I'll give you the gun and you can do whatever you want with me."

"How do I know you won't just start blasting once he's gone?"

"Guess you'll just have to trust me."

Boss glared at him, clearly not happy with that answer.

"My patience is running out," Jack rasped. "You don't start untying my son in about three seconds, I'm just gonna start shooting and take my chances." He paused, returning Boss' glare. "So what's it gonna be?"

Boss held his ground, unflinching, and for a moment Jack felt like David facing down Goliath. When over ten seconds ticked by without the giant mutant moving, Jack figured he would have to back up his tough words with hard action and shoot his way out. His finger applied slight pressure to the shotgun's trigger, getting ready to make his move. He didn't know how he and Kevin would get out of this alive, but he was sure of one thing—no matter what happened in the next few moments, he was putting the first shotgun blast in Boss' ugly face.

Boss must have sensed he was on the brink of having his brains blown out, because he suddenly motioned for Cyclops to let Kevin go. The one-eyed monster snarled in protest. Boss barked at him, some bestial grunt that seemed part command, part threat. Whatever it was, it completely cowed Cyclops, who immediately lumbered over and cut the ropes binding Kevin to the poles.

Kevin flopped on the ground, eating a mouthful of dirt in the process. He laid there for a few moments, his tortured joints burning as if they had been filled with molten lava. Then he summoned his strength and stiffly rose, stumbling over to his father.

"Dad, you don't have to do this," he said. If you had asked him yesterday if he cared if his father lived or died, the answer would have been an emphatic, "Hell, no." Now that his dad's death was a stark possibility, he suddenly realized he didn't want to lose him. He might not be perfect … but he was still his father.

Jack used one arm to keep the shotgun aimed at Boss and used his other arm to pull Kevin to him, hugging him close. He put his mouth next to his son's ear and whispered, "Yeah, I do. But don't worry, I'm not going down without a fight."

Kevin whispered back, "There's more guns back at the lodge. Hold these fuckers off until I come back for you."

"I'll do my best. Now go."

Reluctantly, Kevin moved away from his father. He stared daggers at the mutants, paused long enough to spit defiantly at Boss' feet, and then ran up the nearest trail as fast as his aching legs would allow. Just before he slipped between the boulders and into the woods, he turned and looked back at his dad. An unspoken apology passed between them and Jack nodded as if to say, *I know, son.*

Swallowing the sudden lump in his throat, Kevin nodded back, then vanished into the woods.

"Your boy's safe … for now," Boss grunted.

"Time to pay up. Put down your gun."

Just because Jack was *willing* to die for his son didn't mean he was in a rush to do so. He began backing up, saying, "Sorry, I'm having a change of heart. Think maybe I'll just hold onto this here gun and be on my way." He retreated another step.

Boss bared his teeth. Jack could see scraps of meat stuck between the yellowed incisors. "Better think twice about your next move," the mutant leader warned.

"Yeah? Or what." Jack took another step back.

The ground collapsed under him as the thin screen of twigs and leaves covering a punji pit—a large hole bristling with sharpened stakes—broke beneath his weight.

He flailed, trying to keep his balance, but it was too late. His leg plunged into the pit. A stake impaled his ankle, another stabbed through the meat of his calf. Hot pain blazed through him as muscle fibers ruptured beneath the stakes' merciless penetration. He toppled backwards, dropping the gun in the process.

"Or that." Boss moved in and kicked the shotgun out of Jack's reach. It skidded across the ground and came to rest in a pile of bleached bones. He motioned to Mongus and

Cyclops, and the hulking savages surrounded Jack. They dragged him from the pit, the stakes ripping apart his leg in bloody spurts, ragged chunks of meat clinging to the sharpened wood like shish-kabobbed morsels ready for a cannibal barbecue.

Jack was tossed to the ground and the three mutants immediately began stomping the shit out of him. Their heavy boots smashed into his face, crashed into his skull, and thudded against his ribs. Just before he blacked out, Jack heard the distinct sound of his own bones breaking.

And then nothing but merciful darkness.

CHAPTER 7

DEATH COMES RIPPING

Kevin made it back to the hunting lodge in record time despite the thorns that clutched and scraped at him every step of the way as if trying to slow him down. He slammed through the front door, tore off the knife-slashed shirt that hung in rags from his torso, and threw on a flannel shirt. Next, he grabbed a scope-mounted shotgun from the rack on the wall and slung it over his shoulder.

There was a shelf full of ammo boxes beneath the gun rack. He loaded the shotgun with twelve-gauge slugs and then shoveled as many shells into his pocket as he could fit. He didn't know how many he would need to save his father, but when it came to bullets, too many was always better than not enough.

He bolted from the cabin and raced back up the trail.

******

Jack brutally regained consciousness when Mongus jerked him to his feet by his arm, yanking the shoulder out of the socket. Cyclops did the same thing with his other arm, another sickening crack causing Jack to shriek. The vicious stomping had left him weak and broken; only the support of the two mutants kept him upright. He looked like he was on a cross, arms stretched out, feet together, and shoulders slumped, head hanging limply.

Wicked eyes gleaming with predatory fire, Boss picked up the barbed-wire-wrapped logging chain they had planned to use on Kevin, took up position behind Jack, and with a vicious snarl began scourging his back. The mutant leader's massive fists wielded the metal-barbed chain with the ease and skill of a Roman centurion filleting a condemned criminal with a cat o' nine tails.

The first few lashes tore Jack's shirt to

ribbons. The next few lashes did the same thing to his back. Blood spurted from the deep, flesh-ripping lacerations. And the blows kept coming. Pain beyond anything Jack had ever known slammed through his body.

Against his will, he screamed.

******

Kevin sprinted down the trail, boots occasionally slipping on frost-coated rocks, threatening to turn an ankle and hobble him. His lungs burned from exertion, but he continued his manic run through the thorny brush back to the mutants' cabin.

Off in the distance, his father's screams shattered the morning air into frozen splinters of aural agony.

Kevin felt his heart contract as if clenched by a cold, painful fist. He picked up the pace, sprinting desperately toward his dad's terrible cries. *Not again*, he thought as his boots pounded the earth. *I can't lose another parent to a killer.*

He ran toward the father he had thought he hated, knowing that he would do whatever it took to save him. *Hang on, Dad, I'm coming.*

******

Boss let the blood-dripping logging chain drop from his fist to fall in a coiled heap like a metal snake. The mutant leader wasn't even breathing hard from the exertion of scourging Jack. Mongus and Cyclops let go of Jack's arms and he collapsed on the ground, his back shredded into raw hamburger. Glimmers of bone glistened wetly in the mangled mess.

Boss walked over to the large wooden cross, where the skeletal remains nailed to the wood grinned down at him in a death's head grimace. Boss pulled the whole thing out of the hole—rotting carcass and all—and lugged it back over to where Jack lay prostrate. He let it fall to the ground in a billow of dust and dirt, the desiccated skeleton rattling from the jarring impact. Only the spikes kept the bones from falling off the cross. But when Boss began to kick at the flesh-stripped skeleton, the bones broke free and scattered everywhere until nothing remained on the rough-hewn crucifix.

The wood didn't remain bare for long. Boss and Mongus dragged Jack onto the cross. He was far too weak from blood loss to even try resisting. Splinters from the cross scraped across his whipped-open back like a cheese grater and he nearly blacked out again from the pain.

Unconsciousness would have been a mercy. Consciousness was living hell.

Right now, hell ruled the day.

Jack was dimly aware of his wrists and ankles being bound to the cross with barbed wire. The realization that he was about to be crucified filled him with terror, but the beating and scourging had robbed him of any ability to fight back.

He didn't even scream when Cyclops hammered the stakes through his hands and ankles.

Jack felt himself being lifted as the mutants tipped the cross back into its hole. As the cross dropped back into the ground, the impact slammed his nearly-exposed spine against the cross' vertical beam, ripping an agonized gasp from his lips. The sound seemed to be music to the mutants' ears as they stepped back and marveled at their torturous handiwork; their jagged-toothed grins showed their pleasure at what they had done.

But even in the midst of hellish pain, Jack's prayers were not for himself, but for Kevin. *Please, God, keep my son safe from these sons of bitches.*

Not the prettiest prayer ever prayed, but definitely one of the most earnest and heartfelt.

Jack somehow found the strength to raise his head and look up into the sky, as if to make sure his plea reached the heavens. *Just stay away, Kevin,* he thought. *Don't come back for me.*

And then his body, overloaded with pain, could take no more. Sweet, merciful unconsciousness rushed over him. His head fell forward as blood pooled at the base of the cross.

******

Inside the cannibal's cabin, the woman in the cage stood and stared out the window at the man nailed to the cross. This was hardly the first crucifixion she had witnessed, but this one hit her harder than most. Tears trickled down her filthy cheeks as she said to Mr. Brown, "Oh my God, I think I know that guy."

Mr. Brown didn't respond. The woman turned and looked at the spider's web.

It was empty. Mr. Brown wasn't there.

She felt a brief moment of panic. But when she turned back to the window she noticed something moving across the ground, a small dot of darkness journeying over the white frost. Mr. Brown had exited the cabin and was now outside, scuttling over the rocks and bones, making its way toward the dying man on the cross.

It looked like a spider on a mission.

******

As Kevin neared the ridge overlooking the cannibal's cabin, he stopped running and dropped onto his stomach. Heart pounding, he slithered through the last few yards of brush until he found an opening that gave him a view down into the hollow.

He brought up the shotgun and looked through the scope to assess the situation. He wanted nothing more than to charge down there and try to blow the mutants to hell in a gun-blazing rescue attempt, but he knew such recklessness would only get both him and his father killed. Better to pause a moment to gather information and formulate a proper plan. He just hoped he wasn't too late.

That hope died in a withering wave of horror when he saw his father nailed to the cross.

For the first time in a lot of years, Kevin felt tears sting his eyes. "Oh my God. Dad ... no..."

He brushed away the tears and then peered through the scope again just in time to see a huge spider crawl up the blood-stained cross and settle on his father's shoulder. It paused for a moment, then turned away and sidled up to his dad's ear, putting its two front legs right on Jack's earlobe. Kevin knew his mind was playing tricks on him, but he would have sworn the spider was actually *talking* to his dad.

Jack suddenly lifted his head and looked directly at Kevin, who felt a chill run through him. There was no way his father could know that he was up here on the ridge, but he looked right at him anyway. The spider darted back down the cross, hopped over the pool of blood, and raced back to the cabin.

Through the scope, Kevin locked eyes with his father, even though he knew his dad couldn't really see him. At this distance, it was impossible for Kevin to hear what Jack was saying, but the scope's magnification allowed him to see the movement of his father's lips.

To read his father's final words.

"I love you, son."

Kevin felt his heart break. He set down the shotgun and pounded the ground with his fist, punctuating each impact with a whispered, "No, no, no, no," through grief-clenched teeth as tears streamed down his face. He choked back sobs as he picked up the gun and tucked his eye to the scope to look at his dad again.

Jack's body drooped on the cross with the finality of death, limp and lifeless as it hung from the nails.

Rage rose up inside him to add fire to his grief, but before he could do anything about his turbulent emotions, he felt the cold, hard barrel of a gun press against the back of his head.

A gruff voice said, "Sorry to intrude, son, but I ain't got time for your blattin'. Need you to roll over real slow and don't even think about having a go at me with that there shotgun or I'll blast a blowhole where your head used to be."

Kevin hesitated. He didn't know why—with a gun to his head, it wasn't like he had any options—but instant compliance just wasn't in his genetic makeup.

The gruff voice said, "You're thinking bad thoughts, boy, the kind of thoughts that'll get the top of your spine blown out the front of your teeth. Now roll over, real slow like. Won't ask you again."

Kevin slowly obeyed, rolling onto his back, keeping his hands well away from his shotgun. He looked past the .30-.06 bolt-action hunting rifle aimed at his face and focused on the man wielding it. He suddenly realized he had seen the man before. "I know you," he said.

The man nodded. "Big Bad Bill's the name and guns are my game," he said. "Kind of like the one I got right here. At this range, it would blow you right in half, so don't try no funny business, you read me, son?"

"I'm not your fucking son."

"With your mother rotting six feet under and your dad so recently deceased, looks like you're nobody's son," Bill said. "Now let's go. I know you already met my boys, but I think a more formal introduction is in order, then you can all get reacquainted."

"Your boys? You mean those … *things*?"

"That's right," Bill said. "My boys. So watch your mouth when you talk about 'em."

"Those sons of bitches killed my father," Kevin seethed. "Nailed him to a goddamn cross."

Bill chuckled. "Yeah, they do that sometimes. Couldn't tell you why. Makes you feel any better, he won't go to waste. Now let's go."

Bill marched Kevin down into the hollow, the muzzle of the rifle never straying far from the middle of his back. He seriously considered making a suicide play right here and now.

Even though it would probably end with him getting shot dead, he would bet his last dollar that death by a bullet would be preferable to what these monsters had in store for him. But he decided to wait and hope that an opportunity with a higher chance of success presented itself somewhere down the road.

Of course, it looks like I'm running out of road.

Despite the coldness of the morning, when they passed his father's crucified corpse, the flies were already swarming on the fresh meat. Kevin turned away, but there was nothing he could do to stop the loud, insectile buzzing that invaded his ears as the flies feasted on his father's mangled flesh. Kevin wasn't really sure what he believed about life after death, but he prayed that wherever his father was right now, he could only hear angel-song, not this hellish buzzing.

Kevin clenched his jaw as fresh tears burned his eyes.

Bill paused to stare up at Jack's tortured body. "Ya know, kid, I heard all them stories 'bout your dad being a gutless coward and, well, honestly, I kind of believed 'em. But I reckon I may have misjudged, because it's pretty obvious that in the end, your dad actually did have a spine." He chuckled cruelly. "Look, you can see it from here."

Furious, Kevin whirled around, only to find the muzzle of the rifle touching the tip of his nose.

"Cut your shit, boy," Bill warned, "or I'll blow a brand new asshole where your fuckin' face used to be."

Kevin saw that Bill's finger had taken up nearly all the trigger slack. It would only take another ounce or two of pressure to turn the man's harsh threat into gruesome reality. Kevin defied the gun for a few tense heartbeats, staring defiantly into Bill's eyes. But when Bill's finger twitched on the trigger, Kevin decided he wasn't yet ready to eat a bullet. He let his gaze drop and resumed walking to the cabin. He felt like a condemned man marching to the execution chamber.

When they reached the cabin, Bill shoved him through the doorway so roughly that he stumbled over the threshold and nearly did a face-plant on the filthy floor. Bill followed him inside and called out, "Look what I caught, boys!"

The three grotesque mutants had been hunkered over a table, cauterizing Mongus' wrist stump with a blowtorch. Kevin's stomach churned at the reek of charred flesh and a black, meaty smoke hung in the air like a miasma.

It smelled like the devil's barbecue.

Upon seeing Kevin, Mongus immediately growled and reached for his axe with his remaining hand. His eyes blazed with hatred like scorching hot coals burning in the smoke.

"Put it away," Bill ordered. "Playtime comes later."

Mongus continued to glare fury at Kevin, but did as commanded and set the axe down.

Bill looked at Boss and said, "Put him in the cage with that one-armed bitch. And you—" He looked at Cyclops. "—go fetch his would-be hero of a father off that damn cross and bring him in. We've got some work to do."

Cyclops lumbered out of the cabin while Boss tossed Kevin into the cage as if he was nothing more than a rag doll. The door was then slammed shut and padlocked.

Kevin knew he should be feeling hopeless and afraid, but right now the only emotion he felt was total shock as he stared at the maimed and filthy woman trapped in the cage with him. But it was not the shock of revulsion—it was the shock of recognition. "I know you," he said.

The woman nodded. "Yes, you do." Her

voice was dry and coarse, as if rusty from lack of use, spilling over chapped, cracked lips. "I'm Holly Wainwright. Pastor Wainwright's daughter."

Kevin couldn't believe it. "Holy shit!" he said. "You're supposed to be dead!" A sobering thought suddenly struck him and he took a hard, serious look at his surroundings, then asked, "*Are* you dead? Am *I* dead? Is this … Hell?"

"I'm not dead and neither are you," Holly said. "Not yet anyway. And no, you're not in Hell. But you are in a world of hurt."

"They killed my father."

"I know. I'm sorry. Not that it helps, but I know how you feel. They killed mine too."

Kevin blinked at her, confused. "What are you talking about?"

"My dad," Holly said. "Pastor Larry. When they took me, they killed him."

"No, they didn't."

Now it was Holly's turn to blink in confusion. "What?"

"He's alive," Kevin said. "He's fine. What made you think he was dead?"

"They told me they killed him," she said, pointing at the cannibal crew who seemed to be listening to their conversation with bemusement.

Kevin curled his fingers through the links in their cage and gripped it tightly as he glared at Bill and his three mutated sons. "Guess that makes them liars as well as murderers."

Holly seemed to be struggling with the revelation that her father was alive. A lot of different emotions played out on her face. "I've been here for two years. If he's alive, why hasn't he come for me?"

Bill walked over to the kennel and kicked at Kevin's fingers. He pulled them back just in time to avoid having them crushed by the heavy boot. The whole cage rattled. "I believe I can shed some light on that subject," Bill said.

Cyclops chose that moment to crash through the door carrying Jack's corpse over his shoulder, his shredded back on full display, arms and legs dangling limply to reveal the nail holes in wrists and ankles. Kevin turned his head away and shut his eyes, but he couldn't shut his ears. He winced as he heard the thump of Jack's body being slammed down on the cutting table.

Kevin opened his eyes again just in time to see Bill grin and let out a bellowing whoop. "Fire up the fryin' pan!" He donned a blood-spattered apron and grabbed the biggest meat cleaver Kevin had ever seen. He wielded it with practiced ease, as indifferent as any butcher slaughtering a cow or hog. The fact that it was a human body he was cutting up seemed to bother him not a whit. Meat was meat and bone was bone and the cleaver carved through both like a razor.

Bill talked while he worked. "The reason Larry hasn't come for you is because unlike this cowardly piece of shit here—" The cleaver smashed into the body again. "—Larry actually cares whether his family lives or dies and he knows the second he tells anyone about us, your ass is deader than a blind skunk trying to cross a six-lane highway at rush hour."

He flipped something into the frying pan and Jack's severed fingers started to sizzle. Kevin felt his face blanch but forced himself to stay strong. He couldn't afford to break down in front of these sons of bitches.

Bill continued chopping and chatting. "Larry also knows that if he stops sending us fresh meat, you're dead. It's a supply and demand kind of world. We make the demands, your daddy is the supplier."

Holly slipped her fingers between the links of the cage and gripped them tight enough to turn her knuckles white. Beneath the grime, her face was just as pale. "What are you saying?"

"The day we snagged your perky little ass, instead of deep-sixing you and your dear ol' dad right there on the spot, we struck a deal with him," Bill said. "A deal with the devil, so to speak. At least, I'm sure that's how he figured it. He shuffled on back to town and told everyone you were dead. We even gave him a finger from another woman, a previous visitor, and put your class ring on it to help sell the story."

Bill paused for a moment as the cleaver got stuck in a thick section of femur. Grunting, he yanked it out, then resumed talking. "Of course, that story was a bunch o' bullshit. Truth was, we kept you alive and in return, Larry keeps sending people our way. Every time someone mentions they'd like to go for a hike, commune with nature, he suggests here. Whenever a couple needs some alone-time, he offers them the lodge. Every time some sissy-ass father and his derelict son need to bond, he suggests a hunting trip to Scar Lake. You getting the picture yet? Your daddy sends us lambs for the slaughter and in return, we don't slaughter his little lamb."

Holly looked horrified. "No, not my father

… he'd never … *never* do something that evil. He couldn't."

"He could, he can, and he does," said Bill. "You'd be surprised what someone will do in the name of love." He put down the cleaver and picked up a filleting knife, using it to point at Jack's body. "Case in point right here."

Bill put the knife to use, slicing off chunks of flesh. He started with the meatier parts, methodically stripping them off the bone. Some of it went into the frying pan, some of it went in the kettle. Sautéed or boiled, Kevin knew it would all soon go in their bellies.

Trying not to focus on the desecration of his dad's body taking place right in front of him, he asked, "Why do you do it?"

"Do what?" Bill didn't even look up as he ran the knife completely around Jack's neck to separate his head from his body.

"Why do you eat people?" Kevin winced at the sharp crack as Bill snapped his father's spine.

"Because we're hungry, boy, that's why," said Bill. "Love to give you a more existential answer, but when it's all boiled down to brass tacks, that's pretty much it."

Kevin stared daggers at the man. "You assholes ever heard of a fucking grocery store?"

Bill stopped cutting and pointed the knife at Kevin. A ruby red morsel of raw meat clung to the tip. "Let me tell you something, boy, I came to these here mountains before there were towns, before there were Mickey Ds and Burger Kings and cafes on every corner. And back then the winters were hard. Not sissy hard like they are now, but true hard, man-killers. Back then, if a man didn't want to be murdered by Mother Nature or wasted by Old Man Winter, then a man did whatever he had to do in order to survive. That's what it's all about—survival."

"What a bunch of bullshit," said Kevin. "You're trying to tell me you've been around since the end of the 1800s? That the kind of smoke you're trying to blow up my ass? That'd make you, what, at least a hundred and twenty years old?"

"I ain't trying to tell you anything, boy. But I will say this: you'd be amazed what regular exercise—" Bill held up the knife with a chunk of Jack on the tip. "—and a healthy diet can do to prolong a man's life."

He popped the knife in his mouth and slurped off the meat. The blade went in crimson and came out clean. He chewed loudly, mouth open, deliberately tormenting Kevin and Holly. They both shuddered as he swallowed the flesh with a noisy gulp.

"Fountain of youth right there, kids." Bill let out a contented sigh and smacked his lips. He positioned Jack's severed head in front of him, picked up the cleaver again, and raised it overhead. "Time to make head cheese," he quipped, and then slammed the cleaver down, chopping Jack's skull in half. Brain matter spilled in soggy clumps from the split bone.

Kevin slumped in a corner of the cage and watched in grief and revulsion as Bill finished butchering and cooking his father. He didn't want to look, but he couldn't look away either. He owed it to his father. He had been a dick to his dad and now his dad was dead. Had willingly sacrificed himself so that Kevin could live. Kevin felt obligated to watch every moment of that sacrifice, including the final violation of consumption by the cannibal pack.

Bill and his boys gathered around the table and tore into the meal with something close to religious fervor. No utensils; they went about their morbid feast with bare hands, shoveling chunks of Jack's vivisected body into their mouths as if it was the last meal they might ever have.

Mongus picked up a finger, snapped in half, and slurped off the flesh. He gagged for a moment, then reached into his mouth, pulled out a fingernail, and flicked it toward Kevin. It hit the floor and tumbled to a stop just outside the cage. Kevin stared at it. Soon that fingernail would be the only thing left of his father. Nails and bones.

"See, son, I told you he wouldn't go to waste." Bill popped a piece of Jack's heart between his greasy lips, chewed slowly for a few moments, then said, "Maybe you would understand better if I told ya how it all began. Sit back and let me tell you a story."

CHAPTER 8

THE BEGINNING

Bill knew his wife Hettie was half an idiot—hell, probably closer to three-quarters—but he loved her anyway. Still, just because he loved her dearly didn't mean her constant crazy cries didn't rub his nerves rawer than a scrotum dragged over rusty metal.

"Jesus is coming to take us away, Bill!" Hettie shouted. "He's damned upset with us. That's why I can't have a baby!"

Her babbling cries bounced off the walls of their tiny one-room cabin. She lay in bed, her torso riddled with a hellish rash, and the smell of excrement polluted the air. Bill had grown accustomed to the stench. Good thing too, because he was pretty sure it was permanently ingrained in the log walls. Bill changed her when he could—a loathsome job that proved how much he loved her—and usually had to burn her clothes, the filth too foul to be cleaned from her garments.

She'd been talking nonsense for weeks.

Some of it was the disease, of course. But most of her delirium stemmed from the fact that she was starving.

They both were.

Not for the first time, Bill cursed himself for settling this deep in the Adirondack Mountains. What had seemed like a splendid idea in the heat of summer now seemed like the height of idiocy in the frozen clutch of winter. They were young, newly married, and shared a mutual disdain for their fellow man. They had wanted to be alone, in the middle of nowhere, able to start and raise a family in solitude and seclusion. Hence the reason they had chosen such a remote location to call their home.

But what they hadn't planned on was a winter so harsh and vicious it would kill or drive out all the wild game in the area. Scar

Lake was an inhospitable region during the mild seasons; during the winter, inhospitable turned to nearly uninhabitable. Day after day Bill went out, trudging through waist-high snow drifts until he was exhausted, but couldn't find a deer or hare or squirrel or anything that would make a meal. Hell, if he could have located a bear's hibernation den, he would have crawled in after the beast, that's how desperate he was to find food for him and Hettie.

For months and months their only sustenance was the corn they had brought with them when they settled here. It should have been enough to last them an entire year, but they hadn't counted on the lack of game. Winter had struck early and hard and the game had vanished and the snow had closed the pass they used to get to town. They were trapped here until spring.

Now, because they'd eaten nothing but corn for months, it was almost gone.

Bill knew if he didn't find something to eat, he and Hettie would be dead by spring. It would be months, maybe even years, before some traveler found their bones. There would be no Christian burial, no one who would mourn their passing. They would just cease to exist.

And if starvation didn't get them, then the disease would. Bill wasn't exactly sure what the malady was called, but he had heard about a sickness prevalent in the southern states that impacted women and children because of poor diet. Men were less susceptible to it, which was why he wasn't as ill as Hettie, but even he wasn't completely immune. Starvation and disease ... either one on its own was enough to kill them. Combined, it felt like he should abandon all hope and just wait for Death's scythe to harvest their souls.

He walked over to Hettie with a cup of water in his hand, but she was asleep. He smiled down at her affectionately and gently touched her cheek, careful to avoid scraping his knuckles against the open sores on her nose. She was not what anyone would call a pretty woman at the best of times and this damnable disease had made her even uglier, but he loved her completely.

He told her so while she slept. "I love you, Hettie," he whispered. "I'm going to get us out of this. We are going to make it. I swear to you, we will make it through this godforsaken winter."

He said it with such conviction, he almost

believed it himself.

Quietly, so as not to wake her, he donned his coat and boots, covered his face with a piece of cloth, and grabbed his banged up Henry lever-action rifle from where it hung on two nails in the wall. He turned back for one last look at Hettie, glad she was asleep so she couldn't see the desperation in his eyes, and murmured, "Wish me luck."

As he opened the door and stepped out into the snowstorm, he silently prayed. *Please, God, let me find something for us to eat.*

Outside the world was white. He could barely see the trees through the thick, choking snow. He cursed the blizzard and the howling wind snatched away the profanities. He needed to hunt, needed to find something, anything, for them to eat. But he dared not stray far into the forest for fear he'd be lost in the storm. The best he could do was walk in a circle around the cabin, no more than fifty yards in the woods, keeping the structure in sight so he wouldn't get lost in the blinding snow and brush and be forced to rely on his mental compass. As he slogged through the drifts that seemed to grow two inches with every passing minute, he knew he was wasting his time and depleting his strength for no good reason. It would take a miracle to find game this close to the cabin, especially in the middle of a blizzard.

Sorry, Hettie. Looks like I'm gonna fail you again.

After an hour, Bill slumped against a tree. Clumps of snow broke free from the branches and dumped all over his head. His hands and feet were freezing. He needed to warm back up before venturing out again. He would do neither him nor Hettie any good by getting frostbite.

As he pushed away from the tree, he heard someone shout, "Hello! Is there anyone there?" It was a man's voice, deep and throaty and coated with fear and barely audible above the howling wind.

Bill cupped his hands around his mouth and yelled back, "Who's out there?"

No reply, but moments later two people—a man and a woman—emerged from the brush. They were covered in snow from hat to boots and appeared to be on the verge of collapse. Bill almost missed them; their snowy clothes made them little more than blurry ghosts in the blizzard.

Where the hell did they come from?

"You there," said the man, teeth chattering.

"Do you have shelter? We got turned around in this blasted storm and then our horse died on us. We thought we were heading toward town, but somehow we ended up here instead. Can't even tell you how long we've been out there, but we're pretty close to freezing to death."

"Town's twenty miles south of here," Bill said. "You would have never made it. Not sure how you made it up here, either, 'cept by the grace of God."

"A miracle indeed," the man agreed. "The Lord does provide for His children."

Bill pointed toward his cabin. "Follow me and we'll get you inside and warmed up."

The woman said, "Thank you, good sir."

Bill led the way, breaking a fresh path through the snow until they arrived at the front door of the cabin. But as he reached for the handle, he suddenly hesitated. Inside was his beloved Hettie, covered in sores and shit and delirious with starvation. She would be mortified at the thought of strangers seeing—and smelling—her that way.

"Is there something wrong?" the man asked.

Bill turned and faced him. "It's my wife, Hettie. She's deathly ill. She wouldn't want anyone to see her like this, especially strangers.

I'm sure you can understand."

The man took a step closer to Bill and said, "Yes, I can certainly understand that. But you have to understand that if my wife, Grace, doesn't find shelter soon, she'll die." He patted his rotund stomach. "She doesn't hold up in the cold as well as someone as large as myself." He chuckled as he said it, but Bill distinctly heard the panic in his voice. He also saw how the man's hand crept beneath his coat.

"Sorry," Bill said, "but I think I'm gonna have to ask you to leave."

Grace gasped. "Oh, please, no!"

"'Fraid so."

"You're sentencing us to death," the man said.

"Yeah, sorry about that."

The man's eyes suddenly went desperate and dangerous. "And I'm sorry about this." He whipped a knife out from under his coat and lunged at Bill.

Bill had been expecting something like this. He sidestepped the slashing attack and kicked the man in the side of the knee. The leg buckled. Bill chopped the rifle butt across the man's chin, splitting the skin to the bone. The man spun around and landed on his back in the snow.

When he tried to sit up, Bill shot him in the head. The heavy .44 round sent the back of his skull spraying into the blizzard.

He turned to Grace, who was just standing there with her mouth hanging open in horror. No need to waste a bullet on her; he slammed her in the forehead with the butt of the rifle. She fell onto the snow next to her dead husband. Bill wasn't sure if she was dead or not, so he made sure by bashing her skull into broken chunks. She was a frail little thing, so it didn't take that many blows.

"When I tell ya to leave, I mean it." Bill spat on the corpses, wiped the clotted gore off his rifle stock, and then went inside the cabin.

He found Hettie wide awake and bawling like a baby.

Bill set his gun on the table, kicked off his boots, and shrugged out of his coat. "What's wrong, honey?"

She smiled at him, the big, stupid grin of someone half crazy, as tears of joy raced down her cheeks. "You got something, didn't you, Bill? You finally found something other than corn for us to eat. I heard you shoot, Bill. Please, dear, I need to eat something right now or I'm going to die. I can feel it and God came to me in a dream and told me so…"

Bill sat down on the bed and put his arms around his wife. "Not sure how to tell ya this, Hettie, but … I thought I saw something out by the shed and I fired at it. But there was nothing there. Just the snow playin' tricks on me."

"No, Bill." Hettie pushed him away. "Don't do this to me. Just … don't. You cannot keep telling me that we don't have anything to eat." Her voice was low, but hysteria crept along the edges. "I married you and you said you'd take care of me." She blinked at him, then suddenly screamed, "Look at me! Is this how you take care of your wife?" Spittle flew from her dry, cracked lips and spattered his face.

"I'm doing everything I can," Bill said. "Do you think I like feeling this helpless?"

She pointed at the door and hissed, "You get back out there and find me something to eat."

"Hettie, it's a blizzard out there."

"I don't care!" she shrilled. "I don't care, I don't care, I don't care!" With every "I don't care," she pin-wheeled her arms, slapping wildly at him.

Bill moved away from her crazed attack, shrugged back into his wet coat, and slipped his feet into his cold boots. He picked up his Henry rifle and steeled himself to once again wage war with the wind and snow. He paused with his hand on the door, the wood cold to the touch. Head lowered, not looking at his wife, he said quietly, "I love you, Hettie."

There was no reciprocation of the endearment, just a dire warning. "Bill," Hettie said, "you either come back with something for me to eat … or don't come back at all. I mean that with every ounce of my being."

With a sinking heart, Bill opened the door and walked out into a white, snowy hell.

******

He returned an hour later lugging a large slab of meat. As he kicked the door shut behind him, he smiled at Hettie and said, "We ain't having any corn tonight. Hope your chompers are working, 'cause you're gonna be sinking 'em into something juicy."

He fired up the stove and dropped the bloody meat into a pan.

"I knew you'd come through for me, Bill," Hettie said. "Praise Jesus and all the saints. What is it?"

"Does it matter? I found it out in the snow, frozen to death, so I cut off a chunk and brought it back. Good news is, there's enough there to last us at least a week or so."

Hettie clapped her hands like a happy baby just given a new toy. Bill heard her stomach growl from all the way across the room, even over the sharp sizzle of the cooking flesh. "I don't care what it is," she said. "I just can't wait to eat it."

Bill didn't waste time cooking the meat very long. Rare, medium-rare, well-done … none of it matters much when you're starving. He grabbed a plate, cut off a large hunk, and brought it to Hettie. She squealed happily and the sound made Bill smile. She ignored the fork and picked the meat up with her bare hands, lifting it to her mouth and tearing off a huge chunk with her yellowed teeth.

"Good Lord, what is this delicious meat? I've never tasted anything like it." Drool spilled from the corners of her mouth and trickled down her chin as she took another bite.

Bill stood next to her bed, ravenously shoving the food into his mouth. Between bites, he muttered, "I don't know. Like I said, it doesn't matter."

"And you said there's more?"

Bill nodded. "Not a whole lot more, but it'll keep with the cold weather out there. It's March already, by my figuring, so the storm has gotta break soon. And then maybe the game will come back, or we can get to town if we need to."

She smiled at him with lips soaked in meat juice. "We made it, Bill. I knew we would."

Bill leaned over and kissed her, both of their mouths gleaming greasily in the flickering candlelight. "We did. Now eat."

******

It was almost two weeks before the storm broke. It was like God just suddenly decided enough was enough. One moment it was snowing like hell, the next the sun was breaking through the clouds. Not that it was warm out, or even that nice ... but it was livable.

Hettie put on her coat and said, "Bill, I'm going outside. I'm overdue for some fresh air." She paused and added, "You know, my rash is gone."

Bill winked at her. "I noticed that last night when we were naked."

"Bill!" She waved a hand at him, pretending to be all blushed and embarrassed. "You know," she said, "I cannot believe how different I feel."

Her transformation had been remarkable. Just a few days of eating the meat had pretty much cured all her ailments. Bill believed in God and so he believed in miracles ... and Hettie's healing was definitely a miracle. As was the ferocity of their renewed lovemaking. Hettie had always been dutiful in her marital obligations, but since eating the meat, she had been insatiable and Bill went to sleep every night with a drained smile on his face.

"Glad to hear it," he said. "But now that we got you back to normal we need to find more meat. We can't have you going back to being sick. I will never let that happen to you again."

She gave him a bright smile. "I love you," she said, and then went outside.

When she was gone, Bill began pacing the cabin. What the hell was he going to do? Hettie didn't know it, but they only had enough meat for one more meal. After tonight, it was back to the corn. The thought made his stomach churn. He walked over to the cabin's only window and stared out at the snowy landscape, lost in his bleak thoughts. So lost that he didn't even hear Hettie return.

He heard her scream though.

"What did you do?" Hettie's wail was loud and shrill from where she stood in the doorway. Bill turned around to see her holding Grace's crushed head in her hand.

He started to answer—"Hettie, I—" but then she threw the head at him.

It hit the floor with a frozen thud and rolled awkwardly across the boards until coming to a stop at his feet. Bill didn't even look down at; he just stared at Hettie, whose face was pale and white.

"Did you kill those two people?" she demanded. "I found their bones outside. And the other head too."

"What do you want me to say?" Bill stepped over the severed head, walked to Hettie, grabbed her arms, and shook her. "Dammit, woman, you told me not to come back if I didn't have any meat. You were starving to death." He stopped shaking her and pulled her close, clutching her to his chest. "Please, Hettie, forgive me, but at that point it was them or us."

She resisted his embrace, pushing him away. "You made me eat another human being!"

Bill felt his face flush with anger. "Would you rather be shitting yourself every day? Would you rather be covered in sores again? Would you rather be fucked in the head and babbling nonsense? Because that's what would have happened. I saved you, Hettie. It's as simple as that." He turned away from her. "You're fuckin' welcome."

He walked over and picked Grace's head up off the floor. A month ago just the thought of having to touch a severed head would have repulsed him; now it was just a piece of unwanted meat. Sure, he could probably crack open the skull and fry the brains or something, but he wasn't quite ready for that. He opened the door and tossed the head out into the snow.

He put on his coat. Without looking at Hettie, he said, "I need some air. I'm gonna go scout around, maybe down by the brook, see if I can drum up any game. If not, we have to find our way into town soon." He opened the door, then paused. "Or maybe you like eating corn."

He slammed the door on his way out.

******

Hours later, Bill headed back to the cabin, his mood greatly improved. He had found some fox tracks in the snow, spotted a few raccoons, and even glimpsed a beaver perched atop its dam down by the brook. Not that any of those animals were great eating, but it did signify that the lean times were coming to an end.

Meat had come back to Scar Lake.

When he returned to the cabin, Hettie was sleeping again. Bill almost left her that way, not wanting to deal with another fight about the consumption of human flesh that had saved their lives. But he figured hearing the good news about the game returning might make her feel better about what they had done. Sometimes you just had to do whatever it took to survive.

He put his hand on her shoulder, giving her a gentle push. "Hettie," he said softly. "Wake up, honey."

She stirred, yawned, and turned to him. "What is it?"

"The game is back. I found some tracks, even spotted a few critters. Looks like we're going to be just fine."

"Bill, I think I'm pregnant."

Her words jolted Bill as if he'd been struck by lightning. "What? But how? Well, I mean, I know how, but … we've been trying for over a year!"

She smiled. "I'm late, we've been intimate a lot the last couple weeks, ever since I started feeling better. I don't know how to explain it, Bill, but I can feel it. I'm pregnant."

She climbed out of bed and hugged him, eyes bright with joy. Bill picked her up and swung her around, grinning like a fool. "I'm going to have a son!" he shouted.

"You don't know that. Could be a daughter."

"No, it will be a boy."

"Hopefully the first of many," she said. Then she grew serious and changed the subject. "Who are those people who live about five miles down the road? We met them once on the way to town."

Bill had to think about it for a minute. "I think their name was Anderson," he said. "Why?"

"After our fight this morning, after you left, I had time to think about some things. About everything, really." She paused and swallowed hard, as if whatever she was about to say next was going to be difficult. "I … I believe in my heart that the reason my disease went away and why it went away so quickly is because … because of what we ate." The last five words came out in a rush, as if she just wanted to say them as fast as possible and get it over with.

Bill just stared at her. He couldn't believe what he was hearing.

"And more so," Hettie continued, "I haven't

felt this alive in a long time. Alive and *pregnant*, Bill! And it's all because we…" Her voice trailed off as she moved closer to him with a vague look of guilt on her face. She put her hand on his chest and looked up at him. "Please," she said. "Don't make me say it."

Bill patted her hand. "You don't need to say it. Now, if you'll excuse me, I think I'm gonna go pay the Andersons a visit."

She smiled at him. "Come back soon. I'm getting hungry."

******

Nine months later, Hettie gave birth to their first child.

"It's a boy," Bill announced, wrapping the infant in a blanket. He handed the screaming baby to his wife.

Hettie was exhausted from the grueling labor, but she eagerly clutched the child to her bosom. A smile started to appear on her tired face, but before it could fully form, it turned into a frown. "Bill, there's something wrong with him."

He looked down at his newborn son. Studied the deformed head covered in bone spurs and lesions and stared into the strange, misshapen eyes that stared back at him. When the baby opened its mouth to wail, Bill glimpsed teeth already poking through the pink gums. He had never heard of such a thing and it told him that his boy was different.

Bill felt paternal love and pride burrow into his heart. "What are you talking about?" he said. "He looks perfect to me."

Hettie looked down at her baby boy again. "He just looks ... different." Then her frown abruptly broke into a huge smile. "Oh, who am I kidding? He's beautiful."

"Soon as you can, I want to have another one," Bill said. "That baby boy needs a brother. Hell, maybe two or three brothers." Just the thought of sex made his dick twitch. He had become horny as hell—they both had—ever since they had started eating their neighbors instead of shunning them.

"I love you, Bill. More than anything in the world."

Bill looked at his family and felt peace and contentment. As his son cried and his wife smiled, he knew he would do anything to protect them. They were his blood, and he would spill the blood of any who would dare to harm them. There was nothing he wouldn't do to keep them safe, happy, and healthy.

Nothing.

CHAPTER 9

GUNS AND GUTS

Kevin and Holly remained in the cage for the entire day. Bill and his mutated sons feasted on Jack's corpse for what seemed like hours and when nothing but bones remained— cracked open and sucked empty of marrow— they passed around a bottle of homemade moonshine. Morning became noon and noon became night and all they did was guzzle down the rotgut.

Except for Mongus. While the others drank, he just stared at Kevin and used his remaining hand to play with his axe, slowly and methodically running his thumb along the honed edge to test its sharpness. Even as big as the axe was, Kevin had no doubt that the giant could wield it one-handed.

Mongus' patience abruptly expired. He slammed his fist on the table, glared at his father, then pointed at Kevin while grunting madly.

"Fine," Bill said. "Go fetch him and let's get this over with." He let out a long-suffering sigh. "Never figured out why you boys think you need to play with your food before you eat it."

As Mongus stepped toward the kennel, Kevin thought about retreating into the farthest corner of the cage and forcing the mutant to come in after him. But he knew it would be a waste of time, a fleeting delay of the inevitable. So rather than retreat, he met Mongus at the door. As a show of defiance, it was pretty pitiful. But it was better than nothing. If he had to die, he would rather die defiant than die cowering in the corner.

As Mongus hauled him out of the cage, Kevin glanced at his Stoeger shotgun leaning against the wall near the table.

"Thinking about going for it, boy?" Bill taunted. "Thinking that if you can just get your hands on that piece of hot lead hardware, you might be able to save your skin, avenge your dad, and get the girl? That the general idea flittin' through your tiny little brain right now?"

Kevin didn't say anything. He didn't need to. Apparently Bill could read his mind.

"Well, you can think about it all ya want, but for that thought to become reality would take one damn big miracle the likes of which ain't been seen since the loaves and fishes." Bill chuckled. "And in case you ain't noticed, God hasn't exactly been making His presence felt around here in quite some time."

Even in Hell, God is there.

Kevin wasn't sure where the thought came from—probably some snippet of a Sunday school lesson from a long time ago.

He felt himself suddenly lifted into the air as Mongus picked him up and then slammed him down on the cutting table, still damp with his father's blood. Kevin fought, but even his prison-hardened muscles were no match for Mongus' freakish strength. Even though the mutant was missing a hand, he still held Kevin down with ease. The few blows that Kevin managed to land were ineffectual. It felt like he had punched a concrete block.

He heard Holly scream, "Leave him alone!" and turned his head to see her pressed against the kennel, gripping the links with white-knuckled fingers.

Then he focused all his attention on Cyclops as the one-eyed mutant sledgehammered the empty bottle of moonshine and picked up the shards of broken glass. Fear did a fast crawl through Kevin's guts. Cyclops' filthy hand tried to pry open Kevin's mouth and he resisted with everything he had, clenching his jaw so tightly shut that he risked cracking a tooth or two.

Better a ruptured molar than what Cyclops had in mind for him.

Snarling, the mutant grabbed the sledgehammer and raised it high over his shoulder. Realizing he was about to have his lips pulped and his teeth shattered, Kevin abruptly decided defiance might be overrated. "Okay!" he said. "Wait! I'll do it." He opened his mouth as wide as he could to show his compliance. No reason not to. If Cyclops slammed him in the face with that sledgehammer, blood and broken teeth would run down his throat and choke him, forcing him to open his mouth anyway.

Grunting in satisfaction, Cyclops set aside

the hammer and proceeded to cram shards of glass from the broken moonshine bottle into Kevin's mouth. Kevin thrashed his head from side to side as he felt the sharp edges lacerating his inner cheeks. Ropey strands of bloody saliva whipped around his face.

But even through the pain and horror of the violation, there was hate. He wanted to kill these bastards so badly. Kill them … or die trying.

Please, God, just give me one chance.

Turned out that maybe God hated the cannibal mutants too, because Cyclops made the mistake of leaning over Kevin with a gloating grin on his twisted mouth and bloodlust burning in his only eye.

That bulging eye made a damn good target.

Kevin spit the mouthful of broken glass into Cyclops' face with everything he had. His mouth got cut up even more in the process, but it was totally worth it. Cyclops staggered back, screeching—one of the shards had impaled his eye, instantly blinding him. The orb bulged grotesquely for a moment and then popped, a thick, gory sludge oozing from the deflated eyeball.

The rest of the cannibal pack froze for a moment, unable to believe what had just happened. Then Holly pounded her fist against the cage and yelled, "Hell, yeah!" and they all burst into frenzied motion.

With an enraged bellow, Mongus grabbed his axe and swung it at Kevin's head. But Kevin had seized the moment and was rolling off the table. The axe narrowly missed smashing into his skull and thudded into the wood instead.

Moving with the desperation that comes from knowing you are truly screwed if you're too slow, Kevin managed to snatch up his shotgun before anyone could stop him. He pivoted toward Mongus just as the giant pulled the axe out of the table for another swing.

Kevin worked the trigger twice in rapid succession. The first slug caromed off the axe blade, but the second carved a gory crater in Mongus' gut. He staggered backward, dropped the axe, and clutched at his oozing entrails.

Even blinded, Cyclops proved dangerous. He used the sound of the shotgun blasts to home in on Kevin's position. He stalked forward, swinging his sledgehammer crazily in front of him like a blindfolded kid trying to hit a piñata. Kevin pointed the shotgun at the charging mutant but a wild blow from the sledgehammer knocked the barrel to the side as he pulled the trigger. The shot discharged harmlessly into the cabin wall.

Cyclops brought the hammer back around, but this time Kevin was ready. He ducked beneath the blow, felt the rush of displaced air as the hammer passed just above his head. He quickly rammed the shotgun up under the mutant's chin and slammed down on the trigger.

Instant cranial obliteration.

Bill's hand was on his rifle and Boss was reaching for his chainsaw as the rotten sludge that passed for Cyclops' brains splashed against the ceiling.

Kevin trained the shotgun on them. "Don't even think about it, you sons of bitches," he threatened, though he suspected some of the toughness was lost due to his bleeding mouth. Then again, maybe the blood spilling down his chin made him look like a badass.

Whatever it was, Bill and Boss seemed to get the message, because they both stopped in their tracks. Still, Bill didn't seem all that alarmed. "In case you can't count, boy," he said, "you've only got one shot left and there's two of us."

Kevin shifted the shotgun so it pointed directly at Boss. "So I'll put a slug through his fuck-ugly face," he said, then swung the Stoeger toward Bill, "and then I'll shove this shotgun up your ass until you're tasting gunmetal on your tonsils."

"I suggest you put down the gun and maybe, just maybe, I'll think about letting you walk out of here alive," said Bill.

"The only thing that's gonna be put down is you," Kevin said. "Now let Holly out of that cage and everyone gets to live to die another day."

Bill shook his head. "Not happening."

"Then you're dead. Simple as that."

"Soon as you pull that trigger, my boy here will be on you like stink on shit. He'll rip your arms off and beat you to death with them."

"Maybe. But you'll still be dead."

Bill cocked his head and studied Kevin. "You're tellin' the truth, ain't ya, boy? I can see it in your eyes, plain as day. You're in a killin' mood."

"You sick bastards killed and ate my father. Doesn't exactly take a genius to figure out why I want to blow your brains out your ass." His mouth burned with pain and all the blood seeping from the lacerations was making it hard to form words. "But what I want right now is for you to let Holly out of that damn cage."

Bill turned to Boss and said, "Do it," before turning back to Kevin. "You won't get far. You know that, right? These are our hills, our woods. We'll hunt you down in the dark and when we get you back, what we do to you will make what we did to your father look like a fuckin' pillow fight."

"Reminding me of what you did to my father might be hazardous to your health," Kevin said grimly. His finger tightened on the trigger. He really wanted to blast a hole through Bill's face. *If only I had two slugs left instead of one.*

Boss walked over to the kennel and opened the door.

"Now back away," Kevin ordered.

Boss complied, but his glare made it clear that if ever got his hands—or chainsaw—on Kevin, there would be no mercy.

Holly stared at the open door for a moment, as if unable to believe what was happening. She probably felt like a damned soul who has suddenly found an escape hatch out of Hell but is too afraid to take it for fear it might just be an illusion designed to give birth to hope …

and then brutally crush it.

Kevin was just starting to think she really wasn't going to leave the cage when she suddenly scrambled out, flinging tufts of filthy straw into the air behind her in her haste to exit her prison.

As she ducked through the kennel's opening and stood up, a huge fist reached out and grabbed her ankle. She shrieked and looked down. Despite the big hole in his belly, Mongus wasn't done dying yet. His hand clasped around her ankle as he started to pull her to him.

Kevin feared he would have to use his last shot to save her—which would actually be the death of them both—but she managed to kick herself free and ran to stand behind him.

"Well, well, well," Bill sneered. "A scared little punk and a one-armed preacher's whore. Won't exactly be the most challenging hunt we've ever been on."

Kevin heard Holly open the door behind them and began backing toward it, keeping the shotgun trained on the cannibalistic killers. "I'd think long and hard about that hunt if I was you."

"You ain't me," Bill said.

Kevin paused in the doorway. "Just

remember that sometimes the hunter is the one who gets fucking killed."

He slammed the door and together he and Holly ran from the cabin.

CHAPTER 10

A DEAD RECKONING

Kevin and Holly fled toward the woods, knowing that any minute Bill and Boss would be after them like hounds after hares. As they passed the bloody cross, Kevin spotted his knapsack lying on the ground and scooped it up without breaking stride. He slung it over his shoulder as they passed between the huge boulders and entered the thick, unforgiving forest.

"What's our plan?" Holly asked, panting. Just the short dash across the clearing had left her nearly out of breath. Not a good sign.

"The plan? Run like hell," Kevin said.

"Good plan."

They put the plan into action, fleeing through the woods in a desperate, pell-mell dash that ignored the limbs that whipped them and the thorns that scratched them and the roots that tripped them. But it soon became apparent that Holly could not maintain such a pace. She gave it her best, but after a few minutes of running blindly through the dark woods, she collapsed against a tree, heaving for air like an asthmatic having an attack. Her fingers dug into the bark as she grimaced in pain.

Kevin ran several more yards before realizing she had stopped. He trotted back to her and lightly touched her shoulder. "Are you okay?"

She shook her head, still trying to catch her breath. Every time she exhaled, her breath plumed fog-like in the cold night air. Finally she said, "Have to … rest. Been in that … cage … for two years. No … exercise." The words came out in staggered huffs. "Lungs … ain't … what they … used to be."

"Holly, stopping isn't really an option. Those bastards can't be far behind us." Kevin scanned their surroundings but all he could see was moon-lit darkness and twisted shadows.

"Sorry … no choice. Have to … rest." She raised her head and looked at him. "Leave me … if you have to."

Her eyes were luminous in the moonlight.

Despite everything—the death of his father, his mangled mouth, the fact that they were being hunted by genetic freaks who wanted to turn their bodies into all-you-can-eat buffets—Kevin found himself drawn to her.

He gently touched her cheek and said, "That's never going to happen."

They held the fragile moment for a few seconds that Kevin refused to think of as wasted, and then he moved away, a plan formulating in his brain. Just off the trail was a large, decaying log that would nicely serve his purpose. He opened his knapsack and pulled out a hunting knife. He had planned on field dressing a deer with it, but if this plan didn't work, he and Holly would be the ones gutted.

"You still believe in prayer?" he asked.

He expected her to hesitate—how could she not, given all that she had been through?—but she answered immediately. "Yes. Why?"

Kevin walked over to a tree and hacked off a four-foot-long branch. "Because you might want to fire one off right about now."

"Something wrong with your lips?"

"Yeah. A giant-ass mutant motherfucker rubbed broken glass all over them." He grinned at her for a second, exposing blood-stained teeth, then grew sober. "Guess I'm just not much into God these days. Kind of surprised you still are, after all the shit you've been through."

"How do you think I got through all that shit?"

He stared at her for a moment. Her faith was impressively unshakeable. Kidnapped, tortured, presumably violated in ways he didn't even want to think about, her arm amputated … and yet she continued to believe. He wouldn't have been surprised if she told him that her favorite Bible verse was, *Though He slay me, yet will I trust Him.* He shook his head and started stripping the leaves off the branch.

As he worked, he said, "Just so you and I are clear, if we make it out of this alive, I'm going to kill your father." He didn't look at her as he said it. Just kept his head down, whittling away at the branch.

"If we make it out of this alive," she replied, "I'm going to ask you not to."

"My father, all those other people … all dead, all because of him. I should just let him get away with it?" Two more strokes of the knife and the branch was tapered to a sharp point. "I don't think I can do that."

Holly didn't respond. Maybe she knew that

GRISTLE

nothing she could say would change his mind.

He held the branch up, inspecting the spear. The freshly carved wood almost seemed to glow bone-white in the darkness.

"You have a problem killing one of those things?" he asked.

Holly shook her head. "I think we're a little past the whole 'turn the other cheek' thing."

"Good." Kevin pointed to the decaying log. "Get in."

He hid the spear beneath some leaves as she crawled inside the log, then joined her. The darkness was as black as the devil's soul, the only light coming from the moon cutting through a knothole the size of a half-dollar. Kevin quickly sketched out his plan and then they waited in silence.

It wasn't long before they heard twigs snapping and leaves crackling as something heavy stomped through the woods with all the grace of a bull in a china shop. At the other end of the log, Holly waited. Kevin wondered if she was holding her breath like he was, not wanting to betray their position. For his plan to work, timing was everything.

He heard footsteps right outside the log and then saw something long, slimy, and worm-like dangling in front of the knothole—a loop

171

of Mongus' intestinal tract. It looked like someone—Bill, most likely—had hastily sewn up the shotgun wound in Mongus' abdomen, but some of the stitches had ruptured, allowing the intestine to slither free. The mutant seemed to be ignoring the greasy, flopping tendril as he clutched his double-bladed axe and peered into the darkness, searching for his prey.

Mongus took another step forward, putting him just past the knothole.

Now or never, Kevin thought.

He tapped Holly's ankle. She instantly let out a loud cry and bolted from the log like a scared rabbit flushed from cover. Kevin could almost hear her thoughts. *Come on, you ugly bastard, take the bait.*

Mongus roared and lunged at her with his axe raised.

Kevin powered to his feet, the rotten wood exploding around him as he burst from the log like an avenging angel being born. Mongus reacted swiftly to the sudden threat, swinging his axe backward without even turning around. Kevin ducked under the blade in the nick of time and felt a few hairs shaved off his head.

Running on fear and adrenalin, he rammed his hunting knife high into Mongus' ribs, just below the armpit. The blade scraped on bone but still punched through and Kevin pushed it in up to the hilt, digging for the bastard's black heart. Blood gushed out all over his hand as he twisted the knife. Mongus howled and dropped the axe.

Holly snatched the spear from where it was hidden beneath the leaves. Gripping it firmly, she whirled around. Mongus' mouth was a gaping hole of pain. Holly ran forward and plunged the spear right into the screaming maw, putting enough force behind the thrust that the spear popped out the back of Mongus' head, the sharpened point dripping with gore.

Mongus staggered backwards, clutching at the wooden pole skewering his skull. His ankle caught on a root and he toppled to the ground. He twitched for what seemed like forever but was probably just a minute or two, then finally laid still.

Kevin looked down at the giant corpse, taking in the gut wound, the knife hole, and the punctured cranium. He shook his head in amazement. "Talk about one hard to kill son of a bitch."

Holly came over and stood beside him. "Are you sure he's dead?"

Kevin picked up Mongus' axe and chopped

his head off.

"We are now," he said.

He leaned over to yank his knife from Mongus' ribcage.

The headless body suddenly sat up, clutching at Kevin. Strong fingers gripped his shirt and started pulling him down as blood jetted from the neck-stump, spraying him with a red fountain. Kevin recoiled from the blast of hot, wet gore and threw himself backward. There was a harsh ripping sound as his shirt tore, leaving behind a scrap of cloth in Mongus' clutching hand.

In something close to a hysterical frenzy, Kevin swung the axe again and again and again, hacking and slicing and chopping at the body. *Die!* he thought every time sharp steel thudded into moist flesh. *Die! Die! Die!* He didn't stop until the axe had severed every limb from the torso and then reduced that torso to a quivering pile of meat.

When he was sure that Mongus would not rise again, Kevin stopped chopping. He dropped the axe, sleeved blood and sweat from his face, fished his knife out of the pile of blood and guts, and retrieved the shotgun from the log.

He looked at Holly. "Now that son of a

bitch is dead."

"I'm not going to ask if you're sure," she said.

He glanced back the way they had come. "There's still two of them left, so we have to keep moving. If we can make it back to the Jeep, we can get the hell outta here."

They hustled through the woods, not running, not walking, but a pace somewhere in between, which was about as fast the terrain would allow. They had gone several hundred yards when Holly suddenly asked, "Do you have the keys to the Jeep?"

"Don't need them."

"Then how do you plan on starting it?"

Kevin paused for a moment to catch his breath. Well, more to let Holly catch hers. He leaned against a tree and gave her a smile. "Learned a few tricks in juvie. How to use toothpaste to cut through steel bars. How to make a shank out of toilet paper. How to make sure you never drop the soap in the shower. Oh, and how to hotwire a car. All we have to do is make it to the Jeep in one piece."

"Little late for that," Holly said wryly, looking pointedly at where her left arm used to be.

Kevin wanted to slap himself. *God, I'm such*

a stupid idiot sometimes. Aloud he said, "Holly, I'm so sorry, I didn't—"

She waved away his apology. "It's okay, Kevin, I'm just messing with you." She stepped forward and put a hand on his shoulder. "Really, it's all right."

Their eyes met and lingered for a moment. Kevin was struck by the fact that, beneath all the grime caking her face, she was a very attractive woman.

He abruptly looked away. There was no time for those kind of thoughts. Maybe later, but first they had to get out alive.

******

A quarter mile behind them, Boss stumbled upon Mongus' chopped-to-chunks remains. They were kind of hard to miss since they were so messily strewn across the trail. Boss gripped his chainsaw in one massive hand and canted it over his shoulder as he stared down at his brother—or rather, what was left of his brother—for a few moments. His face was expressionless and had anyone been watching, they would not have seen even a flicker of emotion in his eyes. Finally, he reached down and picked up Mongus' double-bladed axe. No point in letting a good weapon go to waste.

He stepped around the butchered carcass and studied the ground beyond. He was an expert tracker and it was clear which way the boy and the bitch had fled; the scuffed dirt and overturned leaves were practically neon signs glowing in the night.

With an axe in one hand and a chainsaw in the other, Boss continued his hunt, heading toward the Wainwright cabin.

******

Holly was definitely out of shape, but Kevin couldn't hold that against her. Kind of hard to maintain a good exercise regimen when you're locked up in a dog cage. When she started lagging again, he took her hand and practically dragged her behind him.

"Just leave me," she said more than once.

And every time she said it, his reply was, "Not a chance in hell."

The forest was not their friend. Thorns reached out to snag their clothes and slow them down. Roots rose up to cause them to trip and stumble. Limbs whipped their faces and blinded them with watering eyes. But no matter what happened, Kevin never let go of Holly's hand.

Until he banged his head against a hanging

log and then tripped over Vicky Parker's severed leg.

He twisted as he fell so he landed on his back, his arms reaching out to cushion's Holly's fall. She landed on top of him so they were chest to chest, their faces just inches apart. It might have turned into a tender moment if they both hadn't spotted Vicky's crushed head laying just a few feet away from theirs.

Holly gasped and rolled away. Kevin jumped to his feet and pulled her up. Maybe it was his imagination, but he would have sworn her hand stayed in his for a moment longer than was necessary.

He examined the scene for a moment, then handed Holly the shotgun. "Hold this."

She took the weapon from him. "What are you doing?"

"I've got an idea." Kevin removed the leg from the bear trap and tossed it into the brush. He then picked up the trap, slinging it over his shoulder by the chain. He winced as the metal clanked and had no doubt their pursuers could hear it loud and clear, the sound carrying easily through the cold night air.

"Care to explain your idea?" Holly asked.

"Yeah," Kevin replied. "Let's go find a

teeter-totter."

******

Kevin figured he could have reached the teeter-totter in about thirty minutes, but Holly couldn't move as fast as him, so it took the better part of an hour. Sixty long, tense, gut-wrenching minutes not knowing if or when their tormentors would pounce out of the shadows. Dawn was at least an hour away and darkness still blanketed the woods.

They risked stopping only once, at the Wainwright hunting lodge. Kevin ran inside and grabbed a box of shells for the shotgun. He swallowed a lump in his throat when he saw all his dad's hunting gear still strewn about the place. Hard to believe that just twenty-four hours earlier they had been climbing out of bed, ready for a day of deer-hunting. So many deaths since then … and none of them had been deer.

His ammo supply replenished, Kevin exited the lodge and him and Holly finished making their way to the giant teeter-totter without incident. He was surprised to see the crushed remains of the salamander still smeared into the ground. He would have thought some scavenger—raccoon, coyote, fox—would have scarfed up the carrion as a meal.

He left the crushed creature where it lay as he quickly set up his ambush. Winded and one-armed, Holly couldn't really help much, but Kevin found solace in her presence. He had been through hell, lost so much, and there was comfort in knowing he wasn't alone in this fight.

With the site prepped, he made sure the teeter-totter log was positioned so that one end was angled above the trail, then he and Holly hid in the thicket that concealed the other end. If Boss or Bill stepped under the log, Kevin could quickly slam it down on their heads and hopefully put an end to this nightmare.

If they didn't step under the log … well, then he would go to plan B.

They were silent while they waited. Neither of them wanted to take the chance of their hunters hearing them.

They didn't have to wait long.

Holly's reached out and grabbed Kevin's arm tightly when Boss appeared, his hulking frame cutting through the patches of moonlight. The giant mutant paused in one of the patches and raised his nose, sniffing the air like a wolf seeking the scent of blood on the breeze. He carried the chainsaw and axe as easily Kevin would carry a Frisbee.

Come on, Kevin mouthed silently. *Keep coming, you bastard.*

He hoped the humanoid predator wouldn't hear the sound of his heart banging in his chest.

Boss moved further up the trail, then stopped just short of the teeter-totter. Kevin saw him tilt his head down to gaze at the crushed salamander, then tilt his head up to look at the log jutting overhead. Then he snorted in derision and growled, "Ain't gonna be that easy, kids."

He stepped off the trail around the teeter-totter's point of impact, shaking his head as if unable to believe they had actually thought he would put himself in such obvious danger.

His right foot stepped directly into the carefully camouflaged bear trap. Kevin had anticipated that the mutant would sidestep around the teeter-totter rather than walk under it and had placed the trap accordingly.

The metal teeth snapped shut, shearing through flesh and biting into bone. Blood pulsed onto the cold ground. Boss snarled in pain and his eyes burned with rage. The hunter was not used to being outfoxed by his prey.

Kevin and Holly emerged from the thicket.

Despite the emotional trauma he had suffered, despite all the grief and exhaustion and thorn-scrapes and hammered mouth, Kevin couldn't help but feel a sense of triumph as he approached Boss. The mutant stopped struggling and fell silent, glaring at them as they walked toward him. His ugly face expressed hatred, but not fear. But Kevin didn't care about that. He didn't want the son of a bitch afraid.

He just wanted him dead.

"Hey, asshole," Kevin rasped. "I've got something for you."

He shoved the barrel point-blank into Boss' face and pulled the trigger.

The pre-dawn darkness lit up momentarily as fire and smoke engulfed Boss' head. A hole the size of a quarter appeared above his left eye as the slug ripped through his skull. The exit wound in the back of his head was closer to the size of a fist. Bloody sludge flecked with bone bits sprayed across the leaves.

The impact of the shotgun blast to the brain knocked Boss backward and he toppled to the ground clumsily, leg still caught in the jaws of the bear trap. The chainsaw and axe fell from his hands as his leg twisted apart. The steel teeth finished sawing through the limb, snapping the tibia bone and completely severing the appendage. Boss sprawled lifelessly in the dirt as blood jetted from the torn stump in hot gushes.

Kevin and Holly stood side by side, shoulders touching, and watched silently as the gushes turned to spurts and then the spurts finally slowed to a trickle.

Holly stared down at the subhuman beast that had tormented her for so many years. Kevin wondered if she was reliving her abuse or simply relishing the destruction of the abuser. In a quiet voice she asked, "Are you sure he's dead?"

Kevin walked over to Boss and kicked him in the shoulder. He thought about stomping the mutant's head to mush, but Bill was still out there somewhere and he didn't want to waste the time. "He's dead," he said. "Let's go. Just a little further and we'll be home free."

They headed down the path toward the parking area at a fast march. Above them, the black sky started the cyclic process of turning to gray as dawn began to force its will upon the night.

By the time they emerged from the woods at the trailhead and walked out into the parking area, the moon still hung full and bloated above them, but the stars had faded and the heavens were the color of cold ash. Daylight was not far off.

We did it, Kevin thought. *We survived the night.*

But the row of vehicles parked nearby gave mute testament to those who had not. His father's Wrangler. Wayne and Vicky Parker's Blazer. The Rickson's F-150. A Jeep, a Chevy, and a Ford, all bound together by one common trait—dead owners.

Kevin closed his eyes to fight back tears. He missed his father more than he could have ever imagined and he would weep uncontrollably when the right time came. But not now, not yet.

As if sensing he needed a moment alone, Holly walked away, heading for the Wrangler. "You said the Jeep is yours, right?" she called over her shoulder.

Kevin nodded. "Yeah." *Get a grip, Kevin. Now's not the time for tears.*

Holly tried to open the passenger door, but it wouldn't budge. "It's locked," she said.

Kevin took a deep breath to compose his emotions, then walked over to the driver's side of the Jeep, flipped the shotgun around in his hands, and used the butt to bust out the window. He then reached in through the shattered glass and hit the unlock button.

He grinned at her as he pulled his own door open. "Try again."

She climbed into the Jeep and rolled her eyes at him. "Seriously? You learned how to hotwire a car but not how to pick a lock?"

He shrugged. "The guy who knew how to jimmy locks didn't like me much."

"Why not?"

"Because I broke his damn jaw." Kevin ducked under the steering column and used his knife to pry off the cover. He then yanked out a spaghetti-like mess of wires, found the ones he needed, and started stripping them.

Holly asked, "Did you at least have a good reason?"

Kevin sat up and smiled wryly. "Let's just say I like to shower alone." He twisted the wires together and the engine rumbled to life. He pumped the gas, relishing the roar of the motor. "Now that sounds like sweet, sweet music," he said as he reached over and hit the headlights.

Holly screamed.

Boss stood in front of the Jeep, bathed in the bright glow of the headlamps that harshly scoured his rage- and pain-twisted features.

His left leg was half gone and the hole in his head oozed black muck, but somehow he was still alive.

And he still had the chainsaw.

Holly screamed again as Boss raised the weapon above his head and hit the throttle. Exhaust smoke billowed into the night as the injured mutant hopped awkwardly but determinedly toward the Jeep.

"Oh, you have got to be *shitting* me." Kevin dropped the transmission into Drive and stomped on the gas. As the Jeep shot forward, he screamed, "Motherfucker, why won't you just DIE!"

The Jeep rammed into Boss, folding him over the hood. He still clung to the chainsaw and the metal teeth dug divots out of the hood in a shower of sparks. Kevin pinned the gas pedal to the floor as he drove the Jeep right through the sign-in station. He heard the mutant howl in pain and anger as the tiny shack practically exploded, wood shards twisting into the pre-dawn murk like flesh-tearing shrapnel. The Jeep powered through the station and slammed into a massive oak, pinning Boss between the grill and the tree trunk. Kevin couldn't actually hear it, but he imagined the sickening crunch of the mutant's pelvis being crushed. In his mind, it sounded like ice cubes being hit by a hammer.

Boss flopped on the hood, unmoving, and the chainsaw slipped from his grasp. It skittered across the hood and tumbled off the edge, landing on the ground with the throttle stuck wide open.

"Are you sure he's—?" Holly started to ask.

"Don't even say it," Kevin warned, shooting her a look.

He dropped the Jeep into Reverse and backed up, breathing a sigh of relief that driving through the sign-in station and pinning his nemesis against a tree hadn't crippled the vehicle's mechanics. One headlight seemed to be out, but that was it. Boss slid off the Jeep and fell lifelessly to the dirt, landing face-first on the still-churning blade of his own chainsaw. The remaining headlight illuminated the grisly tableau as the steel teeth ripped into the mutant's throat, jaw, and palate before shredding through the brain and tearing his head in two.

"That looked like it hurt," Kevin said as gore spackled the windshield in a chunky mess. He swung the Jeep around and turned on the wipers. The blades whisked away the meatier bits and a few squirts of wiper fluid sluiced away the bloody smears.

The tires sprayed gravel all over Boss' corpse as they drove away. As they headed for the highway in the hopes of putting this hell behind them for good, the first rays of the rising sun peeked over the mountains.

******

Being older and smaller than his offspring, Bill had not even bothered trying to keep up when Boss and Mongus started hunting their escaped prisoners. When his last son died from a chainsaw lobotomy, Bill didn't even know it because he was three miles back at the Wainwright lodge, suffering from a churning stomach.

He paused and leaned against a pine tree, doubled over in pain as a blast of wet gas sputtered from his backside. The painful fart was loud enough to scare birds into flight and set the squirrels to chattering in alarm. He looked at the outhouse and shook his head. "Knew I shouldn't have eaten that liver."

Clutching his stomach, he hobbled across the trail to the outhouse, yanked open the door, dropped his pants with the speed that comes from being desperate not to soil your drawers, and perched his ass over the toilet hole.

He was completely unaware that inside that hole, Mr. Brown was hanging upside down. As Bill loudly voided his bowels, the strange spider crept closer and closer, venom glistening on its unnaturally oversized fangs. Those fangs were deadly pins and Bill's soft butt-cheeks looked like the perfect pincushion.

Oblivious to the danger, Bill yelped, "Oh God!" as he continued the evacuation process, then muttered, "You'd think I ate Chinese or something."

Mr. Brown edged closer, enlarged fangs jutting forward to strike and puncture. The target was close. So close…

The spider pounced forward, slashing with its fangs…

…just as Bill stood up.

Mr. Brown missed by less than a hair.

The spider retreated as Bill stood and wiped, then pulled up his pants and hurried out of the outhouse.

Had he looked back, he would have seen Mr. Brown peering at him over the edge of the toilet hole, all six eyes brimming with an eerie intelligence.

CHAPTER 11

HOMECOMING

By the time Kevin and Holly passed the "Welcome to Vesper Falls" sign, the Jeep was making a strange knocking noise and steam hissed out from under the battered hood. Apparently smashing through the sign-in station and ramming into a tree had done more damage than he initially thought. He would have to drop it off at Twin D Automotive in Saranac Lake to get the engine repaired, followed by some bodywork at Wayne Darrah Auto Body. Assuming, of course, that they had not gone out of business while he was locked up.

But that would have to wait for another day. He knew eventually they would have to go to the police, the hospital, answer a million questions … but not yet. On the drive down from Scar Lake, he and Holly had agreed that before they dealt with investigations and interrogations and evaluations and the inevitable media circus, they wanted some time to themselves, a few quiet moments to catch their breaths. They wanted hot food and hotter showers and a whole lot of sleep in warm beds with clean sheets.

They also wanted to confront Holly's father.

Kevin glanced over at the pastor's daughter. Holly was asleep, slumped down in the seat, her head leaning against the window. He had tried talking to her about how she felt about the horrible things her father had done, but she had remained stubbornly silent. They had agreed to face Pastor Wainwright together, but Kevin had no idea how she would react when the time came. The only thing she had said was, "There's been enough death already."

Kevin almost agreed with her. *Almost.*

Just one more person needed to die.

The sun was cresting over Kate Mountain as they rolled into Vesper Falls. Less than a minute later, Kevin turned into the driveway of his dad's house for the first time in over three years.

Your dead *dad's house,* a nasty inner voice reminded him as he drove up the long gravel driveway that threaded between two large pine trees before coming to a stop in front of the three-car garage. He turned off the Jeep as the first tears streamed down his cheeks.

He had finally come home, but he was too late.

His father was dead.

His mother was dead.

He was alone.

He brushed away the tears and turned his head to look at Holly.

Maybe not all alone.

Holly stirred, realizing the Jeep was no longer moving. She glanced around, then noticed his tears. "Hey," she said, genuine warmth and concern in her voice. "Are you okay?"

He didn't trust himself to speak, so he just nodded.

She unfastened her seat belt. "It's going to be all right," she said. "Come on, let's go inside." She reached over and gently touched his cheek. "Things will get better. I promise."

Kevin looked into her eyes and she looked back. The moment stretched between them. Finally Kevin said, "We should go inside and take a shower."

She arched an eyebrow at him. "Oh really?"

He immediately blushed. "Sorry, I … I didn't mean … we both should take … no, wait … I mean, we both need…" He sighed and gave up. "You know what I meant."

She smiled at him. "Yes, I know what you meant. Just enjoying watching you sweat."

He smiled back, relieved, and then exited the Jeep. Steam still hissed out from under the chainsaw-scarred hood and clumps of dry gore clotted the metal. He shook his head and walked up onto the front porch, Holly following close behind.

Vesper Falls was not the kind of town where you usually locked your doors … unless you had been the victim of a violent home invasion that had left a wife and mother dead. Kevin retrieved the spare key from the hidden compartment behind the "Welcome to the Colters" sign hanging next to the door. Once he and Holly were inside, he locked the door behind them. Given everything he had been through, he suspected he would be locking doors for the rest of his life.

He showed Holly to the master bedroom and pointed toward one of the dressers. "Dad never got rid of mom's clothes, so you can probably find what you need in there."

"What's wrong with what I'm wearing?"

she asked with a smirk.

Kevin looked at the filthy rags and replied, "Nothing that some gasoline and a match won't cure."

He took her into the master bath and showed her where to find the towels, shampoo, and soap. "It's all yours," he said. "I'll use the shower next to the guest room." He closed the bathroom door behind him as he left.

Holly spent a full half-hour in the shower. She had never been one to lie to herself, so she didn't even try to deny the fact that part of her wished Kevin was in here with her. But as the hot water rinsed away the grime and revealed her scarred, abused, semi-emaciated body— not to mention the angry stub of her missing arm—Holly was suddenly glad she was showering solo. She might have been pretty once, but not anymore.

She washed her hair four times and used a whole bar of soap to scrub her body, scouring her skin until it glowed pink. It was a bit difficult with just one arm, but she managed. She made a conscious effort to remind herself that it could always be worse—the cannibal mutants could have cut off both her arms. So as she took her first hot shower in years, she tried to count her blessings rather than tally up her afflictions. She also tried not to think about Kevin in the other shower, tried not to imagine the water streaming over his hard muscles.

What in the world is wrong with me? she wondered. *You'd think after everything I've been through, romance would be the last thing on my mind. Besides, he wants to kill my father.*

She abruptly reached out and turned the shower faucet all the way to "Cold." She stood under the freezing spray until she was shivering and the fires of attraction had been, if not fully extinguished, at least doused into smoldering embers.

She climbed out of the shower, dried off, and then rummaged through Trisha Colter's drawers until she found a pair of underwear. She ignored the skimpy, lacey ones and selected panties that were functional rather than frilly. Sliding them on felt absolutely magical. After dressing in rags for so many years, she had forgotten how comfortable it was to wear good, clean cotton.

She went back into the bathroom and found a toothbrush still sealed in its original package tucked into the back corner of the medicine cabinet, hiding behind a bottle of prescription sleeping pills. Looked like Jack Colter had trouble getting some rest.

Not anymore.

She instantly regretted the morbid thought.

She squeezed some Colgate onto the toothbrush and scrubbed her teeth clean. The bristles made her gums bleed and when she spit into the sink, the white paste was funneled with red. She managed to get the top off the mouthwash bottle and swished some around in her mouth. The antiseptic burned and made her eyes water, but it was a good, cleansing burn.

She found a hairbrush in a drawer and started working through the snarls. She'd gotten some of them out in the shower, using half a bottle of conditioner in the process, but she needed a brush to finish the job. Took her nearly ten minutes—and more than a few winces at some particularly nasty clumps—but she got the job done, her still-damp hair falling smooth and tangle-free down over her shoulders.

Back in the bedroom, Holly picked out a simple white t-shirt and a pair of low-rise jeans. Apparently Trisha had been a few inches taller, so she had to roll up the cuffs. The waist was a little loose, but not too bad, and she really didn't feel like struggling one-handed with a belt.

Before donning the t-shirt, Holly picked out a pink bra and slipped her arm through it. It hung off her shoulder, useless. She realized that putting a bra on when you only had one arm was going to be a real problem. She stood in front of the mirror and tried a dozen times a dozen different ways, but no luck. Finally, she hurled the garment across the room in exasperation.

"Damn it!" she yelled.

She stood there for a moment in front of the mirror, trembling, staring at herself, at her scarred, abused body. She struggled with everything she had to fight down the rage and self-pity that wanted to consume her.

She lost.

"Fuck you!" The scream just suddenly burst out of her. "Fuck you! Fuck you! Fuck you!" She slumped against the wall and wept. Not because she wanted to, but because she couldn't help it. She needed a release and something deep down inside that she couldn't control was going to make sure she got it whether she liked it or not.

She pushed away from the wall and stumbled out of the bathroom, falling face down on the bed and crying into a pillow that smelled of cologne and whiskey.

Footsteps pounded as Kevin raced into the bedroom. "What's wrong?" he asked.

Holly kept her face pressed into the pillow so her words were muffled when she answered, "Nothing. Everything."

"Uh, that doesn't exactly clear things up."

Still not looking at him, she said, "Those bastards made me ugly." She paused for a moment, then added, "And now I can't even wear a bra, thanks to them." Another pause, followed by: "Damn them. Damn them straight to fucking hell."

Kevin walked over and sat on the edge of the bed. He ran his eyes over her naked back, following the curve of her spine all the way down to where it disappeared into her jeans. Sure, her skin was scarred, but he still found it tantalizing. He wanted to reach out and touch her, but decided that might not be the best course of action right now. "You're not ugly," he said. "And you will wear a bra again."

She turned over to look at him, covering her breasts with her arm. "How?"

How is exactly right, Kevin thought. *As in, how the hell am I having a conversation about brassieres with a girl I hardly know who just happens to be topless right now?*

What he needed right now was a cold shower.

"Sport bras," he said. "No straps to deal with. Just pull it over your head and there you go. I'm sure you can manage even with only one arm."

Holly smirked at him. "Look at you, a bra expert. I didn't know they taught that kind of stuff in juvie."

Kevin felt himself blushing. "We were allowed to get Victoria's Secret catalogs."

"Bet they were popular in an all-male facility."

"You have no idea."

She smiled at him. "Thanks for trying to help. By the way, you're cute when you blush."

Kevin was starting to discover that he really liked to see her smile. The lines of hardship etched in her face faded to almost nothing when she smiled, defining her natural prettiness with extra depth. Free from captivity and freshly cleaned, her true grace and beauty shone through. Kevin found himself unable to take his eyes off her. He also found himself not wanting to.

She must have suddenly become aware of his intense stare, because she jumped off the bed, snatched up the t-shirt, and awkwardly pulled it over her head before turning to face him. He saw that she was turning red.

He gave her a roguish grin. "By the way, you're cute when you blush."

"Jerk." But she smiled when she said it and then asked, "Now what?"

"Now I guess we find something to eat, and then…" His voice trailed off and his grin faded as he looked away from her, not wanting to meet her eyes as he finished his thought. "And then we go pay your dad a visit."

There was a long silence. When Kevin finally dared to meet her gaze again, he saw that she was staring at him intently. "Kevin," she said. "I need to ask you something."

"Okay." He dreaded her next words.

She took a deep breath and then asked, "Do you have any frozen pizza?"

Kevin blinked at her. "Really? Pizza? That's what you want to talk about?"

"I don't want to talk about my father."

He stared at her for a moment, then said, "Fair enough. My dad wasn't big on cooking so I'm sure we have pizza in the freezer. Let's go check it out."

******

An hour later, they sat on the couch

watching a rerun of *M.A.S.H.* and munching on DiGiorno's pizza, washing it down with Diet Mountain Dew. A bag of Cool Ranch Doritos on the coffee table in front of them completed the meal.

"I used to hate Diet Dew," Holly said, "but now I think it's the best thing I've ever drank." She picked up another piece of pizza and began gnawing on it. It was her third slice. Skinny as she was, Kevin figured he should probably let her eat the whole thing.

"Yeah, not sure why Dad only had diet soda," he said. "It's not like he needed to worry about his weight." He bit into his piece of pizza, chewed, and swallowed before adding, "You can tell he was a drunk though. Nothing but vodka, whisky, rum, tequila, and something called Rumple Minze in the house." He let out an exaggerated, longsuffering sigh. "All I wanted was a Miller Lite."

"What's Rumple Minze?" asked Holly.

"One hundred proof peppermint schnapps."

"We should try some."

Kevin shook his head. "Screw that. I'm not about to dump hundred proof alcohol into this mouth." He used his tongue to gingerly probe the cuts. "Eating pizza is hard enough. If I had my way, I'd be sucking oatmeal through a straw."

"Don't be a sissy. Do a shot with me."

"Did you just call me a sissy?"

"No, I told you not to be one. Come on, Kevin, I really want to try it."

Kevin shook his head in resignation. "Jeez, you sound like an alcoholic. Fine, I'll go get it." He went back into the kitchen and returned with a bottle filled with clear liquid and two shot glasses. He wondered when the last time the glasses had been used. His father had been more of a straight-from-the-bottle kind of guy.

As he poured, Holly said, "I've never actually done a shot, but from what I understand, they go down the back of your throat. So if you don't want it to burn all those cuts in your mouth, throw it to the back of your throat and swallow at the same time."

He gave her a crooked grin. "Now you sound like a porn queen."

Blushing, she reached for her glass. "And you sound like a pervert. Now drink!"

"Cheers."

They both tossed back the shots. Neither of them really knew what they were doing. Kevin's shot got caught in his throat. He began coughing loudly and stood up, doubled over.

Holly laughed and gave him a few whacks on the back. "Amateur," she teased.

When the coughing fit finally stopped, Kevin said, "See, I told you that shit ain't for me."

Holly grabbed the bottle and poured them each another. "One more. Do it right this time."

"Okay." Without waiting for her, he picked up his shot and slammed it back like a professional. He then set down his empty glass and said, "Your turn."

Holly tossed it back. Apparently her first go-round had been beginner's luck, because this time she started coughing even worse than Kevin had. He slid over and patted her on the back. "Now who's the amateur?" he chuckled.

She leaned over until the coughing spell passed. When she sat back up and turned to him, their faces were kissing close.

So that's what they did.

The kiss was light, hesitant, unsure. Kevin felt Holly freeze up for a second, but when he tried to pull back, she moved into him, kissing harder. It hurt some, but he'd be damned if he was going to tell her to stop. He pulled her close as his hand slid under her shirt, fingers tracing the curve of her spine. He stopped kissing her long enough to nuzzle her neck and softly ask, "Are you sure you want to do this?"

"No," she said quietly. "But we're going to do it anyway."

The combination of double shots and young desire heated up their bodies. Kevin peeled off his own shirt and then helped Holly out of hers. Her breasts were ripe and pert, nipples hard with arousal. He was abruptly consumed by an urgent need to be with her. Call it lust, call it love, call it the desperate need to affirm life in the aftermath of death—hell, call it all of the above. He picked her up, feeling her legs wrap around his waist as he carried her to his bedroom.

Once there, he unsnapped her jeans and lowered her zipper. The metallic rasp sounded loud even over their panting. The jeans slid to the floor and she stepped out of them, leaving them in a puddle of denim on the floor, mute testimony to her need to be loved after years of being abused.

His fingers hooked into the waistline of her panties. "Are you sure?" he asked again.

She leaned in and kissed him, letting her lips linger on his. "I'm sure," she said. "You know we both need this."

He moved his hands downward and her

underwear slid to the floor. His pulse quickened as she stood naked before him, but there was still one more thing he needed to confess. "I've never done this before," he said.

She kissed him again, pressing her body against him. "Neither have I."

Kevin looked at her, surprised. "Sorry, I guess I thought…" He stopped talking. There was no easy way to say it.

"They did a lot of things to me," Holly said, "but they didn't do that."

Kevin undressed and they tumbled into the bed, exploring each other's bodies with an intoxicating blend of sensual hunger and desperate passion. Neither could know for sure what the other was thinking, but they sensed that they both needed the same thing—a few moments of feeling alive, a few moments to ease the pain in their hearts and souls, a few heartbeats of heaven to make them momentarily forget their hells.

Their arousal burned fast and hot as their hands devoured one another. Their moans and gasps echoed through the room as they fully surrendered to the intensity of the moment. Holly moved on top of him and Kevin felt himself immersed in hot, wet silk. He groaned in pleasure and then, as she began to move her hips slowly, uncertainly, he gasped, "My God, Holly…"

It didn't take long. It couldn't, nor did it need to. For a few brief moments, they forgot their nightmares by surrendering to each other, yielding to the satin friction of skin on skin. Their smoldering gazes locked as they moved together until the final seconds came. Then they each closed their eyes as Kevin's shuddering climax rocked them both. She silenced his cry of release with a kiss, feeling the vibrations of his orgasm tremble through him and into her.

"Holy shit," he said when he could speak again.

"Yeah, that about sums it up," she said as she slid off of him and cuddled against his side. He wrapped both arms around her and pulled her close.

"Guess we're not virgins anymore," he said. "Good thing too, 'cause that whole virginity thing was really overrated."

She smiled contentedly and moved even closer to him. "Do you mind if we just lay here for a while?"

"If a while is forever, sure."

They were both asleep in less than a minute.

******

Bill drove back to his sporting goods store in Saranac Lake after spending all day burying his sons in a place he knew no one would ever find them. He hadn't bothered saying any words over their unmarked graves. Heaven … Hell … God would deal with them as He saw fit and nothing Bill could say would change that.

Now he was covered head to toe in dirt, exhausted, and dreading the call he had to make. In some ways, making this call was even worse than putting his offspring into the ground. But procrastination would not spare the pain, just prolong it. He picked up his cell phone, dialed the number, and held it to his ear.

Hettie answered after just two rings. "Hello?"

At the sound of her voice, Bill closed his eyes. He hated the thought of causing her any hurt, but it had to be done. "Hettie," he said, "you need to pack your bags. We need to get outta here, fast."

"Why?"

Bill took a deep breath, exhaled, and answered, "The boys are dead, honey."

He held the phone away from his ear as

Hettie shrieked. The caterwauling lasted a long time, but eventually dissolved into muffled sobs. Bill put the phone back up to his ear in time to hear her ask, "All of them?"

"Yes, all of them," said Bill.

"Even Junior?"

"Yes, even your baby. Sorry, honey. He took a shotgun slug right between the shoulder blades. I buried him with his brothers. Took all damn day."

"I want to see their graves."

"I'll show you someday but that day ain't today," he said. "Today we have to haul ass. Pack your bags and I'll be by to get ya soon."

"Do you know who did it? Do you know who killed our sons?"

"Jack Colter and his boy, if you can believe it. The same yellow-bellied son of a bitch that let me put a bullet in his wife's head is the one who killed your baby and then his boy killed the other three." He shook his head. "Un-fuckin'-believable. Turns out the Colters have more balls than anyone expected. Should have executed the whole lot of them that night instead of just the wife."

"I want you to kill 'em all," Hettie said heatedly. "If my boys are suckin' maggots, I want them suckin' maggots too."

"Oh, you can bet your sweet ass on that," said Bill. "I just stopped by the shop to get a certain gun."

"You mean the gun?"

"Damn straight," Bill confirmed. "I'm gonna drive out to Vesper Falls, execute that fuckin' worthless preacher and his bitch of a daughter, and then I'm gonna shoot Kevin Colter right in the face with the same gun I used to kill his mother."

"Do it for the boys. Do it for me," Hettie said. "I love you, Bill."

"I love you too, darlin'. It's you and me forever—ain't nothin' or no one gonna ever change that. See you soon." He disconnected the call. He didn't want to talk about killing anymore—he wanted to get it done.

He unlocked a drawer, pulled out a Colt .45 with a dragon etched into the walnut handle, and threaded a suppressor onto the barrel. He referred to the automatic as his "thrill-kill" gun, the weapon he used when he invaded homes and killed not for meat, but for pure sport. Slaughtering wayward hikers and lost hunters deep in the woods was nothing more than sustenance; forcing his way into a home in the middle of town and playing his sick, twisted game was pure pleasure.

Unfortunately, in an area as small as the tri-lakes, he had to be careful not to indulge too frequently. He carved a notch into the handle of the Colt every time he thrill-killed and there were only six notches. Trisha Colter was represented by the sixth and final notch. Well, final for now; he would add a seventh notch after he used the gun to put a bullet in her son.

Eye for an eye, he thought. *Sons for sons.*

He grabbed a box of .45 ACP ammo and headed out to finish the hunt.

******

Kevin and Holly slept the sleep of the exhausted, the sleep of those who have been beaten and bruised and battered by life until they are physically and emotionally wasted. Neither of them moved so much as an inch for the next seven hours. Had either of them been capable of conscious thought, the term "sleep like the dead" might have come to mind.

Holly eventually stirred as the evening sun speared through the partially-open shades. She stretched languorously and then nudged Kevin. "Hey, you."

He groaned in response.

She nudged him harder. "Come on, wake up."

Still groaning, Kevin sat up, rubbed his eyes, and announced, "I feel like I just woke from a coma."

"Me too." Holly climbed out of bed, giving him another chance to admire her naked curves. Even crisscrossed with scars, they were very nice curves.

"Where are you going?" Kevin asked, feeling his arousal also awaken. "Come back to bed."

She stood by the side of the bed, just out of arm's reach, and put her hand on her hip. "For what?" she teased.

Kevin devoured her with his eyes. "For … you know."

She smiled, but shook her head and began dressing. "Maybe later. Right now I want to see my father."

Kevin swung his legs out of bed and pulled on his boxers. He suspected their blissful hours of passion were about to come to an end, replaced by grim tension. "Yeah, I want to see your father too." He motioned toward the bed with its rumpled sheets. "I hope you don't think this changes anything. I still want your father dead."

"I know," she said quietly. "I won't lie—I hoped what you feel for me, and what I feel for you, would make you think twice about killing my father, but that's not why I slept with you. That was something we both needed after everything we've been through. But if it had made you change your mind about putting a bullet in my dad, well, that would have been a nice bonus."

He didn't say anything for several long moments. Just stood there and looked at her, eyes hooded and thoughtful. Finally he said, "Let's just see how it goes."

"Kevin…" she started to say, then stopped, biting her lip as her eyes glistened. She turned away to get herself under control and when she looked at him again, her eyes were dry. "No matter what happens," she said, "I have to go back."

Kevin wasn't sure he'd heard her right. "Back?" he echoed incredulously. "Like, back to the cabin?"

"Yes."

Kevin shook his head. "Do you have a death wish? That crazy bastard Bill is still alive and since we killed his boys, I'm pretty sure he wants us dead. Hell, he wanted us dead before we killed his boys." He stared at her, trying to decipher what was going on in her pretty little head. "Why do you need to go back? Why

GRISTLE

would you risk that?"

"I have to get Mr. Brown."

"Who the hell is Mr. Brown?"

"He's my friend," she replied. "My guardian angel. He's..." She hesitated, just for a second, then finished the sentence. "He's a spider."

Kevin blinked. Once. Twice. Then made sure his ears weren't playing tricks on him. "Uh, did you just say, a spider?"

Holly looked hurt. "Don't laugh at me. You can believe what you want, but without Mr. Brown, I never would have survived these last two years. I'm dead serious, Kevin—with you or without you, I'm going back."

He looked at her thoughtfully. "This ... spider ... Mr. Brown ... really means that much to you, huh?"

"Yes, he does."

Kevin leaned over and gave her a gentle kiss. "Okay," he said. "When we're done with your father, we'll go find Mr. Brown."

"Thank you."

He finished getting dressed and said, "I'll wait for you in the Jeep."

Outside, he stood by the driver's side door and looked through the broken window at the shotgun, thinking about what he was going to do to Pastor Larry Wainwright ... and wondering what he would do to Holly if she tried to stop him.

CHAPTER 12

NO FORGIVENESS, KNOW FURY

Pastor Wainwright sat behind his desk as the sun went down, trying to squeeze in some Bible reading before he headed for home to his empty house and a supper that came out of the freezer with microwave instructions on the box. His well-worn study Bible was spread before him, cracked open to the Book of Luke, Chapter Fifteen. The story of the prodigal son, his all-time favorite scripture passage. He had a daughter, not a son, but he still knew what it felt like to desperately wish your child would come home.

He nearly jumped out of his skin as his office door smashed open. The knob banged into the wall with enough force to punch a hole in the sheetrock.

Kevin Colter stormed into the room with a

shotgun in his hands and fury in his eyes. Larry knew at that exact moment that he was a dead man. One look at the coldness in Kevin's gaze and he knew he would find no mercy at the young man's hands. And frankly, he didn't deserve any. The terrible things he had done, the blood on his hands, merited his execution.

Kevin marched across the office and shoved the muzzle of the shotgun right between the pastor's eyes, pressing hard enough that it felt like the skin might split. "Hey, preach," he said. "Bet you're surprised to see me."

Larry kept absolutely still. Sudden moves were ill-advised with a shotgun tucked against his forehead. Just because he knew he was about to die didn't mean he was in a rush to make it happen. The only thing he moved were his lips. "Kevin," he said, managing to keep his voice much calmer than he actually felt, "I must admit this visit is a bit unexpected, but are you sure shoving a shotgun into a man of God's face is the best way to proceed?"

"Man of God." Kevin sneered the words into something twisted and profane. "You've got some serious balls calling yourself that. You set us up, preacher. You sent us out there to be slaughtered by those fucking things and now my father's dead. You hear me? *Dead!* So what you need to do now is give me one good reason not to pull this trigger."

Larry felt like he was going to wet his pants. Never had he been as hyper-aware of his own mortality as he was right now. He searched for the words that might spare him. "You don't understand!" he said, hearing the babbling desperation in his voice. "I didn't have a choice. They have my daughter."

"Had."

"What?"

"They *had* your daughter," Kevin corrected. "Past tense."

"What are you talking about?"

At that moment, Holly walked into the office. "Hi, Dad."

"Oh my God! Holly!" Larry started to rise but Kevin pushed him back down with the shotgun.

"I don't think so," Kevin said. "Sit the fuck down."

Larry complied and once Kevin was satisfied that he wouldn't try to get back up, he moved aside and let Holly approach her father. She walked around the desk, tears in her eyes, and then abruptly threw herself into his arms. For a few moments she was nothing more than a frightened little girl and he was nothing more than her comforting daddy. For a few precious heartbeats their reunion was joyous, sins forgotten, no barriers between them. They wept together as Kevin stood stonily by.

But of course the moment could not last forever. Holly finally stepped back and used her one hand to wipe away the tear-tracks silvering her face.

Larry looked at her with haunted eyes, taking in the emaciation, the scars, the empty shirt sleeve. "Oh, honey, what did they do to you?" Seeing her like this broke his heart. Not seeing her for all these years had almost been easier than having her standing before him now. During her captivity, he had at least been able to imagine that she wasn't being harmed. But now he was forced to face the stark proof that such naïve imaginings had been grossly untrue. Holly's every scar was a stinging condemnation that lanced him deeply.

Holly stared at him and it was plain to see that she was no longer a scared little daddy's girl who needed hugs and solace. That moment had passed. Now she was a survivor. An angry survivor who demanded answers. "Trust me, dad," she said, "you don't want to know what they did to me or what they made me do to them. But what about you? What did *you* do?"

Larry just looked at her. He had nothing to say. There was nothing he *could* say.

"Exactly," Holly said. "Nothing. That's exactly what you did. Absolutely nothing."

Larry thought about reaching out to her, but decided that would probably be a mistake. Instead, he sat still and tried to offer justification for what he had done. "I did what they asked," he said. "I sent them people so they wouldn't kill you. They kept their word, right? Honey, I know they did some terrible things to you, but at least you're alive..." His voice trailed off as he realized he wasn't getting through to her.

Holly looked like she wanted to slap him. "And how many people died to keep me that way?" she demanded. "How many people did you send to be slaughtered and eaten by those ... things ... so I could stay alive?"

Larry bowed his head, tears dripping onto his shoes. "I didn't have a choice, sweetheart."

"Of course you had a choice," she snapped. "You could have tried to save me. His father"—she pointed at Kevin—"saved him. But my father? He did nothing. Nothing! Except send innocent people to be butchered."

Her glare cut into him like a scalpel, as if she wanted to peel back his flesh and peer into his soul to see if there was anything in there worth salvaging. Love glowed in one of her eyes while hate burned in the other and plainly etched on her face was a war between two emotional extremes.

Larry had no response, no words that could make it right. What he had done was unforgiveable. But that didn't stop him from saying, "I'm so sorry, Holly. But please—*please*, baby—can you ever forgive me?"

"I don't know, dad. Part of me wants to, but the other part of me can't forget that you left me in a cage to rot and be tortured by those things." She stared at him, hard and cold, for several long moments before her face abruptly softened. "All I can promise you is this—I'll try. I'll try to forgive you, but it's going to take time."

Kevin broke his menacing silence. "And you might not have a whole lot of that left, preach."

Larry licked his lips nervously and tried to speak. "Kevin, I—"

"Save it," Kevin snapped. "Nothing you can say will make anything right. Nothing will change the fact that because of you, my father is dead. If there were words that could turn back time, I would let you talk. But there's not, so do us both a favor and shut the fuck up."

Holly glanced at Kevin, then looked back at her father with sadness on her face. She leaned down and kissed him on the cheek. "Goodbye, daddy," she said softly, then turned and walked away.

Larry's heart constricted as she headed toward the door, leaving him to his fate. That same heart began hammering wildly as he realized this might be the last time he ever saw her, that just minutes from now, maybe even seconds, he might very well be dead. There was no mercy in Kevin's kill-cold eyes and no chance on God's green earth of surviving a point-blank shotgun blast.

Holly stopped next to Kevin, put her hand on his arm, and said, "I'm not going to ask you to forgive him—I can't ask you to do something I'm not sure I can do myself—but I am going to ask you not to pull that trigger." Her voice thickened with emotion and she swallowed hard. "He's my father, Kevin. The only one I have. Killing him won't bring yours back. It will just leave me without one too."

Her hand slipped away from his arm. "I'll be waiting for you outside."

When she was gone, Larry looked at Kevin, seeing the rage in his eyes. He couldn't imagine what the young man was feeling. First his mother was brutally murdered, then his dad turned into a drunk, then he got locked away, and then days after his release his father got savagely slaughtered. No doubt about it, Kevin Colter had been through some serious hell and Larry was to blame for the latter portion.

Kevin wanted to kill him and even as scared witless as he was, Larry could hardly blame the kid. Vengeance is a normal human instinct and one not easily denied. Larry felt fear-sweat ooze down his face and leave an oily sheen on his upper lip as he awaited the shotgun blast that would send him to his eternal judgment.

Kevin just stared at him, teeth clenched, a vein in his jaw pulsing an angry rhythm. His eyes were colder than a dead viper. He raised the gun and curled his finger around the trigger. But he didn't pull it. Not yet. He seemed to be waiting for something. At that moment Larry realized that Kevin didn't just want him dead, he wanted him broken.

He collapsed into sobs, clasping his hands in front of him in the classic prayer formation as he desperately pleaded with his would-be killer. "Please, Kevin, forgive me!"

Kevin stepped forward and tucked the steel bore of the shotgun under Larry's chin. He levered the preacher's head up and back so that the slug would blow out the top of his skull and paint the picture of Jesus on the wall behind him with red, wet gore. With his lips peeled back from his jagged teeth, Kevin smiled in animalistic rage and said, "Fuck forgiveness."

"NO, WAIT!"

Kevin pulled the trigger.

Larry screamed.

Click!

The firing pin fell on an empty chamber.

Larry soiled himself.

His muscles suddenly failed him and he fell from his chair to sprawl on the carpet as the stench of his shame filled the small office.

Kevin towered above him, the unloaded shotgun canted over his shoulder. "I'll let God deal with you, preacher," he rasped. "Until then, you fucking live with it."

Larry curled into a sobbing mess and it took all of Kevin's willpower not to stomp on the bastard's skull until it broke into tiny eggshell pieces. But in the end, he let him live. Not for his sake, but for Holly's.

As he walked through the foyer toward the front door, he fed four shells into the shotgun. Bill was still out there somewhere and until he was caught or killed, Kevin planned to always have a loaded gun within reach. He had his head down as he pushed open the front door of the church to walk outside, but it snapped up when he heard Holly's strangled cry. What he saw sent fear slamming through him.

Bill stood beside the Jeep, holding Holly hostage in front of him. One arm snaked around her throat like a python while the other hand pressed a gun to her temple.

A gun Kevin had seen before—a Colt .45 with a dragon etched on the grips.

Hot rage joined the cold fear coursing through his veins. His eyes narrowed to angry slits as he locked gazes with Bill. "Where'd you get that gun?"

Bill's face was caked with dirt so his teeth gleamed shockingly white when he grinned and said, "This piece of hot lead hardware? Had it a long time."

"So you're the one who killed my mother." It wasn't a question and Kevin gritted the revelation through clenched teeth.

"Depends on how ya look at it," said Bill. "Way I see it, your father killed your mother by being a pussy, but I guess if ya wanna be all technical about it, then yeah, I put the bullet through your momma's brain."

"I'm gonna fucking kill you."

"Yeah, yeah, yeah," Bill drawled. "Spare me all the threats and tough guy talk. I think we both know how this plays out, right?"

Kevin pulled his eyes away from Bill and looked at Holly. Her face was a mask of fear and her thin body trembled in Bill's grasp. Kevin knew he needed to postpone thoughts of vengeance right now and focus on saving the woman he had come to care for so much. "Let her go," he said.

"We'll see about that," Bill replied. "Kind of depends on you." He waggled the gun without moving the muzzle away from Holly's head. "You see those notches in the handle? Cool, huh? That sixth one is your mother, by the way."

Kevin bared his teeth in a wolfish snarl but bit back the curses he wanted to hurl at the man who had taken so much from him.

"Anyway," Bill continued, "I'm gonna put another notch on this gun today, but whether that notch is for you or for this bitch is entirely in your hands."

Kevin felt his blood run cold. The shotgun was a useless, leaden weight in his hands. With Bill holding Holly in front of him in such a way that less than a third of his head was visible, the shotgun simply lacked the precise accuracy necessary to nail a kill-shot. Someone with more skill might be able to put a slug in Bill's eyeball, but Kevin was not that person. He would more likely just splatter Holly's skull. He couldn't take the risk. He would have to find another way.

Bill ground the muzzle of the .45 against Holly's temple while his other hand reached down and groped her breast, dirty fingers digging in like cruel claws. "I should just execute you right here and then make your boyfriend watch while I fuck your corpse."

Holly whimpered in terror and her eyes sought Kevin, desperately pleading.

Kevin felt horror punch him deep in the guts like an icy fist. Bill's deadly, vulgar threat was too ghastly to even imagine; worse, he knew the man was deranged enough to carry it out. "No," he said. "Please … don't."

"That's up to you." Bill's voice dripped with amused malice. "You see, I'm gonna give you a chance to save your girlfriend."

By now the *deja-vu* was practically palpable and Kevin knew exactly what he was supposed to say, the script he was expected to follow. "I'll do anything you want," he said. "Just don't hurt her."

"Glad to hear it," said Bill. "Now turn that shotgun around and tuck the barrel under your chin nice and tight. Right there above the lump in your throat."

Kevin's mind scrambled for a way out of this mess as he slowly complied. As the gaping bore of the shotgun touched the skin under jaw, right next to a frantically-pulsing vein, desperate horror churned through him. Despite the coolness of the evening, he felt fear-sweat burst from every pore. *I wonder if this is what dad felt like,* he thought.

"Good boy," said Bill. "Now, I think ya know what I want ya to do next."

"Why don't you stop hiding behind a helpless woman?" Kevin taunted. "Let her go, we both put down our guns, and settle this like men."

Bill grinned. "Nice try."

"What's the matter, ain't got no balls?"

Bill's grin abruptly vanished. "I'm gonna bury my balls in your girlfriend's ass if ya don't shut your mouth and pull that fuckin' trigger."

Kevin looked at Holly and for the briefest of moments saw not her face, but his mother's. He vividly remembered the ghastly horror of watching her die. He couldn't let the same thing happen to Holly.

"Do it!" Bill snapped. "Or so help me God, I'll blow her fuckin' brains out."

Kevin knew all too well that Bill wasn't bluffing. He reached down and placed his finger in the trigger guard. With the shotgun turned around the way it was, he would have to push the trigger rather than pull it. Not that it mattered; the result would be the same. He wondered if he would even feel the slug burn through his brain and was surprised to find that he didn't really care. As long as it saved Holly, it would be worth it.

Still, he hesitated, trying to buy some time. As long as there was life, there was hope … hope of finding a resolution that didn't require him to blow his head off.

Holly was staring at him intensely. She couldn't move her head with the .45 pressed against it, but her eyes conveyed a message. *No. Don't do it.*

"Ain't got the guts, hey?" Bill taunted. "Your dad had the same problem. So I'll give you the same incentive I gave him. I'm gonna rattle off a five count. If I reach five and you haven't put a bullet through your head, then I'm gonna put one through this bitch's. Got it? Right here—"

"Yeah, I know the rest." Kevin cut him off. "Right here, right now, I am God. Life or death, the choice is mine. I've heard this shit before, remember?"

Without warning, Bill started the countdown. "One."

Kevin's heart—and his last fragile shreds of hope—sank. He was a dead man. No choice. He would wait until Bill got to four and absent a sudden miracle, he would press the trigger and hope his sacrifice saved Holly.

"Two."

Kevin caught movement in the Jeep next to Bill and Holly. The driver's side window was lowered halfway and a large spider crawled up the inside of the glass. Kevin did a double-take. It looked exactly like the spider he had glimpsed on his father's shoulder as he hung on the cross. Kevin had no doubt that he was looking at Holly's precious Mr. Brown.

Suddenly the doors of the church flew open and Larry Wainwright raced down the steps screaming, "Get your hands off my daughter!" His hair was wild and his pants reeked of shit as he charged Bill with the recklessness of a man who has nothing left to lose.

Two things happened at once.

Mr. Brown reached the top of the window…

...and Bill swung the .45 away from Holly's head long enough to put a bullet in Larry.

Holly screamed, *"NO!"* as her father spun around like a blood-spraying dervish before tumbling awkwardly to the ground.

Kevin saw Mr. Brown hurl itself from the window. The strange spider arced through the air in a gravity-defying leap. It landed right on Bill's surprised face, its eight legs straddling his right eye. The spider immediately sank its dripping, oversized fangs into Bill's right eyeball which popped like a punctured pimple in a spurt of white corneal fluid.

Bill howled like an agonized banshee. He let go of Holly and staggered backward. As she ran frantically to her fallen father, he tripped over his own stumbling feet and fell to the ground, the spider riding his face all the way down. His head bounced off the blacktop with a thud.

Kevin quickly closed the distance between them in several long strides, but as he stood over the cannibal leader, he saw there was no need to rush. Bill's limbs twitched a spastic rhythm as the venom sizzled through his veins and attacked his nervous system. The dragon-etched .45 lay a few feet away, fallen from poisoned fingers.

Kevin tossed aside the shotgun, picked up the Colt, and knelt beside Bill as Mr. Brown moved away, taking up position nearby, watching with eerily intelligent eyes. Kevin could have almost swore the spider nodded in approval as he pressed the muzzle of the .45 under the man's chin, right above the lump in his throat. Bill's remaining eye twitched in its socket as it fixed on him and Kevin relished the fear he saw in the shuddering orb.

"Bad news, Bill," he said. "I'm gonna finish that countdown for you and when I reach five, I'm going to put a bullet in your throat. Right here, right now, I am God. Life or death, the choice is all mine." He smiled grimly. "And you're going to fucking die."

Bill gurgled and white froth spilled from the corners of his mouth.

"One," Kevin said, starting the countdown. "Two. Thr—aw, fuck it."

He pulled the trigger.

The gunshot thundered through the cool Adirondack air.

Bill jerked from the point-blank impact of the bullet ripping through his neck. The muzzle flash scorched the skin around the entry hole a moment before blood jetted from the wound, propelled by air escaping from a punctured esophagus.

Kevin backed away to avoid the crimson fountain and stared down at his dying enemy with vengeful satisfaction as Bill writhed and twitched and choked.

A massive *BOOM!* caused him to nearly jump out of his skin.

Bill's crotch exploded as if someone had slipped a grenade down his pants.

BOOM!

His stomach erupted in a hot, gushing mess of viscera.

BOOM!

His chest came apart in a rupturing burst of torn flesh and shattered sternum.

Kevin whipped his head around to see Larry Wainwright holding the shotgun. There was blood on his side where Bill's bullet had grazed him and he was wobbly on his feet. But his finger was steady on the trigger and hate burned in his eyes.

BOOM!

The fourth and final shot hammered Bill smack in the face and turned his head into something resembling wet dog food.

Larry hobbled over and spat on the splattered corpse. "When you get to Hell," he snarled, "tell the devil the last thing you ate was a fucking bullet."

His legs suddenly gave out. The shotgun tumbled from his hands as he reached out for support. Kevin caught one arm and Holly took the other, bearing his weight.

"It's all right, dad," she said. "We've got you."

The preacher's face was pale but he still managed to smile weakly at his daughter. Blood from his wound—it looked like the bullet might have bounced off a rib—dripped onto the ground.

Holly looked over at Kevin. "We need to get him to the hospital."

"We all need to get to the hospital," said Kevin. "Help me get him in the Jeep."

Working together, they managed to load Larry into the Jeep, stretched out across the back seat. The stench from his soiled pants filled the interior and blood spilled from his wound, but nobody cared. Larry's reckless, sacrificial charge at Bill had been the catalyst that saved the day. He had more than earned the right to bleed all over the leather.

Holly started to climb into the passenger seat, but suddenly paused. "Wait, where's Mr. Brown?"

They looked around but there was no sign

of the strange spider. Holly's eyes searched the entire church parking lot, growing more worried with each passing second, but Mr. Brown was nowhere to be found.

Her shoulders slumped. "He's gone," she said softly with tears in her eyes. "He was with me the whole time. He never left me. But now he's gone."

Kevin put his arm around her shoulders. "I guess all that matters is that he was there when you needed him, right? Maybe you just don't need him anymore."

She leaned into him and smiled. "Maybe I have somebody else."

He pulled her close and kissed her softly. "Maybe you do," he said. "Maybe you do."

They climbed into Jeep and drove away.

Perched on the highest point of the cross that crested the church steeple, bathed in the golden rays of the setting sun, Mr. Brown watched vigilantly until they were gone … and then it went home.

ABOUT THE AUTHORS

Mark Allen writes hard-hitting fiction that slams like a bullet between the eyes or a punch to the guts, but never loses sight of the heart and soul. His writing is tough and uncompromising and he uses words like a scalpel, carving through the surface layers to rip open the bleeding secrets beneath. He currently resides in the Adirondack Mountains of upstate New York with enough firepower and ammunition to ensure he is never bothered by door-to-door salesmen.

Derric Miller writes horror fiction; the darker, the better. He also writes about rock 'n' roll as the managing editor at Hardrock Haven (www.hardrockhaven.net). He's kind of tall too.

70711489R00133

Made in the USA
Columbia, SC
12 May 2017